ANNIE'S ATTIC MYSTERIES®

The
Stolen Canvas

Marlene Chase

Annie's®
AnniesFiction.com

Library of Congress-in-Publication Data
The Stolen Canvas / by Marlene Chase
p. cm.
I. Title
                    2011961134

AnniesFiction.com
800-282-6643
Annie's Attic Mysteries
Series Editors: Ken and Janice Tate
Series Creator: Stenhouse & Associates, Ridgefield, Connecticut

10 11 12 13 14 | Printed in China | 10 9 8 7 6 5

~ Prologue ~

The willowy girl with hair the color of champagne dreaded the summer she would have to spend in the sleepy little Maine backwater, but she would have to endure it.

"It's a lovely place, honey. There's swimming and boating—and a real lighthouse." Her mother patted her face and smiled, wrinkling her newly molded nose. "You'll see; it will be great fun."

The prophecy had proved patently untrue until she met a street-smart girl from Boston who would have been forbidden in the wealthy circles in which her parents moved. She had neither the breeding nor the money so important to them. What she did have was a thirst for adventure and a dinghy with a real outboard motor, which she sort of "borrowed" from an old man who lived up the coast.

Her new friend's mom had "dumped" her there for the summer. And so the two lonely teens had forged a common and devoted bond.

The wiry fifteen-year-old had dark chestnut hair that curled naturally; when it rained it became as kinky as corkscrews. "You can call me 'Corky' if you want to. And you'll be 'Carlotta.' Wasn't she some hoity-toity princess or something?"

"I'm not a hoity-toity princess. Take that back!" the other protested. She was used to being snubbed for being rich, but secretly, she liked the name "Carlotta."

When Carlotta's mom went shopping in the nearby city of Portland with her luxury tour group friends, the girls agreed to meet at the dock. Carlotta pulled on jeans and a halter top, and paused at the mirror. Maplehurst Inn was supposed to be the best hotel in town, but even the double suite her Mom had rented was hopelessly out of date. No television set. No *Charlie's Angels*, and what would the weekend be like without *Saturday Night Live*?

The eventful day was picture-perfect, though whether the girls took note of the climate or not, one couldn't be sure. They did notice the fishermen down at the dock, especially the ones with sinewy muscles and deeply tanned shoulders. The girls sunned near the point, their boom box turned up as loud as they dared. They giggled and chatted over the magazines and candy Carlotta had bought at the gas station on their way to the beach.

When they grew restless, they walked out to Butler's Lighthouse, wandered around the cove, and up and down a country road before heading back toward town. That's when they spotted the car—a sleek silver Mustang Mach 1—its chrome shining with blinding brilliance.

"Will you look at that? A girl could fly to the ends of the earth in that thing!" exclaimed Carlotta. She had never driven a car, and it would be a whole year before she could get a permit to learn. But to go anywhere she wished with the wind blowing through her hair would be heaven.

The car was parked along a shady street some distance from the marina. There were no homes or shops in the vicinity and no other cars. It was as though the Mustang had just suddenly materialized, a magnificent silver horse galloping out of a dream.

Corky, who always pretended that nothing impressed her, shrugged her thin shoulders. When asked how anything was, she would always respond, "boring." Now she craned her head forward and narrowed her eyes.

Carlotta drew in her breath as they stood behind the car. She could feel it like it was something living. The heat rising from the metal, like hot breath against her skin, made her heart pound; she'd never seen anything so beautiful, so powerful. "Someday I'm going to have a car like that!" she whispered.

"Why not now?" said Corky, with studied nonchalance.

Carlotta turned to stare at her. "Sure," she said with a sardonic grin. She shook her head in wonder at the shiny chrome and the racing-horse emblem affixed to the front grill. "This makes my Mom's Caddy look like a museum piece," she murmured. "I'm going to ask for a car just like this for my graduation!"

A click resounded in the summer air. Corky had opened the Mustang's door. They peered inside at gorgeous leather upholstery the color of crimson. The shiny dashboard looked like something out of *Star Trek*.

"What are you doing?" Carlotta stammered. "Are you crazy?"

"We're just taking a look. There's nobody around. Come on."

Someone had left the key dangling from the ignition, as though inviting a test drive. Corky scooted behind the steering wheel. Then Carlotta slid onto the smooth leather of the passenger seat. Impulsively, Corky turned the key, and the engine roared to life. They were off, the automobile lurching and bucking like a wild bronco. The wiry, dark-haired girl drove with high confidence. Carlotta sucked in air as they flew down the dusty roads, the wind tearing at their hair and beach robes.

Neither girl spoke, each feeling the rush of wild abandon. They whizzed along Ocean Drive past the beautiful Victorian home perched atop the hill. In the distance, the peak of Butler's Lighthouse shone in the midsummer sun.

After a while, they changed places. Carlotta tumbled over Corky in her eagerness to get into the driver's seat. She clutched the steering wheel fiercely and pressed her sandaled foot hard on the accelerator. They were one with the wind, the sky, and the ocean. They could drive forever and go anywhere they wanted. Nothing could stop them.

Only something did.

Ironically, the accident didn't happen until their initial frenzy had abated. They had slowed to a crawl, prepared reluctantly to return the car to the place where they'd found it. Carlotta negotiated a U-turn, but the road was too narrow. The tree loomed up in front of them like an alien thing.

Dazed but unhurt, they scrambled out of the car. The left fender was a mangled mess. When the distant wail of a siren sounded, Carlotta ran. She ran harder and faster than she'd ever run in her life. Corky, ashen-faced, seemed immobilized.

It would be hours later before Carlotta learned what happened next, hours before she knew that Corky had been taken to the police station and her mother sent for from Boston. Soon, the truth would come out that she had been with Corky. She had been the one driving and crashed into the tree. Corky would tell them, or someone who saw them would give the terrible details. The police would come for her. Her life would be ruined. Images of reform school loomed over her.

But the police didn't come. When her mother returned from her shopping trip, Carlotta said she had spent the morning alone at the beach and had taken a nap in the afternoon. How easily the lies spilled from her lips.

The following day she learned the worst.

A semitruck driver had fallen asleep while southbound on Interstate 95. Crossing the grassy median, he had crashed head-on into a southbound sedan with Massachusetts plates. Corky's mother never reached Maine alive.

~ 1 ~

Annie Dawson stepped onto the front porch of Grey Gables. Before her, summer lay full blown in shimmering waves of heat. She drew in the scent of the ocean mingled with fragrant rose and lavender. Her gray cat, Boots, scampered past, took a few brief steps and spun around on delicate white paws to regard her. Then, lifting a well-groomed tail in the air, she padded off into the sunshine.

Annie dropped down on a wicker chair, feeling sublimely at home. The sun's fingers cupped her face and wrapped her body in golden warmth. Who would have thought it? She certainly had not expected it when she'd first taken on the estate of her grandmother, Betsy Holden, that repairing the graying old house with its cache of dubious treasures and neglected gardens would turn from duty to pleasure.

She had planned a quick disposition of Gram's things, none of which she needed or wanted—at least not then. She would put the house at 1 Ocean Drive up for sale and go back to Texas. After all, Stony Point was two thousand miles away from her family, and Maine winters were terrible to contemplate, let alone survive.

But she'd done more than survive. She stayed only part of the winter at Grey Gables. She'd reveled in the artful symmetry of the land when snow turned its contours into a wild white sea, and the sun made it sparkle like a faceted diamond. She'd relished walks along the ice-encrusted beach and learned to listen to a silence so deep it felt like a physical presence. She understood now why Gram had been so reluctant to go south in winter. Right up to the end she'd preferred the comfort of her own fireplace and let the elements rage and blow.

Annie had chosen to go home to Texas for Christmas and extended her holiday well past February. Alice MacFarlane, her best friend and childhood companion from summers spent with Gram, had watched over the house faithfully in her absence, and had taken care of Boots. Wally Carson, handyman par excellence, was only a phone call away to check the furnace or pipes. When Annie had come back in early March, winter still clung to the landscape with the tenacity of a white bulldog. While she enjoyed every minute in Texas, she had been anxious about the well-being of Grey Gables.

She had been eager to see her friends in Stony Point too—especially her fellow Hook and Needle Club members. She watched the slow birth of spring and took to Gram's garden with a vengeance. Now the fruits of her labor flowered along the walkway and in the circular gardens she had so patiently dug. Peonies flourished among purple and red salvia; hydrangea and Michaelmas daisies blossomed with unrestrained ardor.

"Good to be home, isn't it, Boots?" She glanced at Gram's gray cat preening her white paws in a patch of sunlight. They'd long since adopted each other but took care not to intrude when one or the other preferred solitude. Now, Boots gave her an indulgent stare, her feline face resembling a smile.

Annie sighed. It wasn't that she hadn't enjoyed spending

time with her daughter LeeAnn, Herb and the twins. She had delighted in the games and banter of John and Joanna. She was delighted to see them in the matching sweaters she had crocheted. She begrudged not one stitch of the difficult design she'd labored over the long year past. She was so proud of the twins; she had soaked up their developing personalities, each so different from the other. Both excelled in school and gave every indication of becoming heads of Fortune 500 companies or even president of the United States. Of course, they'd have to learn their times tables first and grow permanent teeth.

They had been full of questions. "Grandma," Joanna had asked, "what was it like in the olden days?" LeeAnn had giggled behind her hands, and Annie had given her daughter a swat with a towel. *Olden days!* She was only in her forties, for goodness sake. She was no gray old lady yet. And if claiming John and Joanna was the price for being called "Grandma," it was worth it and more.

Serious-minded John, who loved to draw, wanted to know, "Was Gram Holden really an artist?"

LeeAnn had been quick to respond, her blue eyes taking on a proud luster. "She was one of the best! She hand-painted her own canvases and stitched them in the most gorgeous colors you can imagine! Why, she's as famous as Florida's Jane Nichols or Kaffe Fassett of England."

The children had no idea that Nichols or Fassett drew world scrutiny for their original canvases. Still, they seemed suitably impressed.

To illustrate, LeeAnn pointed to the large wall hanging of children playing on a beach. The stitching was so fine and uniform that one had to look closely to be sure it wasn't a grand painting.

It was one of the first major pieces Gram had stitched, a gift to Annie's mother when Annie was born. Annie passed it on to LeeAnn at the birth of the twins. The canvas was large—at least 24 by 36 inches—and needed a large airy spot, which LeeAnn had found in her high-ceilinged dining room. The heirloom was beautifully crafted with a delicate gray-blue ocean in the background and sand in rich hues of gold, brown, and ivory. You could almost feel the warm grains beneath your feet and hear the lapping of the waves against the shore.

"Not many can say they actually own a Betsy Original!" LeeAnn had said proudly.

Annie was surprised at the amount the Hook and Needle Club had raised at the previous summer's charity art fair. The bulk of it came from the auction of Gram's old lighthouse canvas for which a collector had paid $2,000. Inquiries about other New England pieces followed, amazing them all. Gram would be astounded that her canvases had become valuable to anyone but her.

"Hey, dream girl! You ready to go?"

Jolted back to the present, Annie jumped at the sound of Alice's light soprano call. She'd been practically lulled to sleep by warm thoughts of her family.

"Good grief! You scared me!" she quipped as Alice dropped down beside her. "Is it that time already?"

"We'll miss half the Hook and Needle Club gossip!" Alice said lightly. "But Mary Beth won't start scolding until the meeting really begins at eleven. After that, watch out!"

Alice MacFarlane smelled of roses. Her bracelets clinked

pleasantly as she coiled her hands around the arms of the wicker chair. Rings tacitly advertising Princessa jewelry glistened on each well-groomed finger, even the thumbs. Alice's presence only heightened that sense of well-being that had seized Annie from the moment she'd wakened. They had so quickly resumed their friendship; it was great getting reacquainted with Alice's fun-loving ways and to recall long-ago days of sun and sand along the coast.

Summers in the quaint old town of Stony Point, Maine, encompassed some of her most cherished recollections, many of which she shared with Alice.

Grey Gables, the Victorian home of Charles and Betsy Holden, was built on an eastern hill that overlooked the ocean. The spacious lawn gave way to a winding path through wild grasses scrolling down to the rocky shoreline. On the right side of the Victorian house, with its wide front porch, was a small pond alive with tadpoles, creepers, and dragonflies. She'd forgotten how much she'd loved it during those long-ago summers spent with Grandpa and Gram Holden. And now Grey Gables was hers.

"I was just thinking how good it is to be alive," Annie said. "I love to look out at these flowers, these trees, and that magnificent ocean!"

Alice turned radiant blue eyes on her friend and grinned. "Same trees, same ocean as yesterday," she said with a teasing lilt. "Same Miss Philosopher. But we need to get going." Tossing her auburn hair, she tugged at Annie's hand.

"OK, OK," Annie said, rising. "I'll just get my purse and project bag." She went inside, Alice following close on her heels.

"Each time I'm in here, I have to marvel at how you've done wonders with Grey Gables, Annie." Alice crossed her arms over her pale blue shirt and cast admiring glances around the house. "Inside and out! Your grandmother would be so pleased!"

"Well, between the work Wally has done and the work I have done, I guess it looks presentable," she said, scooping up a newspaper and dropping it into the magazine basket. "But you were the one who papered all those hand-cut roses over the vanity in the bathroom."

"It was no picnic either, believe me!" Alice said in mock distaste, and then added, "You've made Grey Gables a showplace that would bring a pretty price. Not that I think you should … well … sell it, I mean." She detoured into the living room. "I've gotten used to having you right next door!"

Annie looked at her friend fondly, recalling that spring she had thought Alice might leave to join her photographer friend, Jim Parker. But the two had shared an on-again, off-again romance, and Alice was still entrenched in the carriage house that was originally part of the Grey Gables grounds. She gave her friend a quick wink. "You just want someone to help you with your parties! Some of them are no picnic either, you know!"

"Is that a new table by the window?" Alice asked.

"That, my dear, is Gram's old Pembroke drop leaf that Wally worked on for me. It must have been quite a chore to restore the inlay."

"Even has a Hepplewhite pull," Alice murmured. "That Wally is a genius with his hands."

"He is that," Annie agreed, "and a sensitive guy too. Did

you know he carries binoculars in his tool chest? He's taken to watching birds, especially when he goes fishing. I bet he could craft wooden birds as well as model boats."

"You got him started on that. I bought one the other day for my nephew in San Diego." Alice stepped further into the room, continued her appraising glances. "Betsy's pillows look great against that dark green sofa cover. Very chic! But maybe you ought to put them under lock and key, now that Betsy Originals are in such demand. That one with the orange poppies is absolutely to die for!"

Crochet tote in hand, Annie paused to stand next to Alice and study the canvas. "It is lovely." She traced the vibrant poppies intermingled with delicate ivy. An intricate border design incorporated the brilliant orange of the flowers and the ivy's verdant green. Annie swallowed the lump in her throat. Gram's unique artistry touched her with singular beauty—a beauty that reflected her life and spirit. And to think she could claim such a heritage for her own.

Annie sighed. She was so richly blessed. The emotion washed over her with such force she felt nearly dizzy. The joy of it all lingered as she rode to town in Alice's sporty Mustang. And soon they were surrounded by the women who had become their friends and confidantes.

The Tuesday morning Hook and Needle Club welcomed women of all ages. From Stella Brickson, who had grown up with Gram, to Kate Stevens's teenage daughter, Vanessa, a bond had been forged among them. They not only shared their passion for needlework but the everyday pathos of living. When Kate went through a divorce after years of enduring Harry's alcoholism, they had all lived through her tears and triumphs. When Peggy Carson's little Emily had been injured, they had showered her with cards, balloons, and visits.

Stella Brickson was just settling herself at the table and caught Annie's eye. "Well, Annie Dawson, good morning to you." In her mid-eighties, she sat ramrod straight, her hair a smooth gray cap on her regal head. She no longer wore it high and coiled with tortoiseshell combs; such a style probably worked havoc with arthritic fingers and aching joints. Still, there was an air of elegance about Stella.

"And to you," Annie answered with a smile. Stella could be formidable when challenged, but she was really a gentle soul. And because Annie had learned that elderly people often missed the tenderness of touch, she put an arm around the woman's soft shoulder and lightly kissed her cheek.

She waved to Gwendolyn Palmer and Kate Stevens who pored over a pattern spread out on the table. Kate wore a pale green jacket embroidered with hummingbirds on each pocket—no doubt her own creation. Gwen, impeccable in dress as in reputation, wore slacks of pale turquoise and a Polo Club knit in petal pink. She and Kate were by far the most dress-conscious of the group, but they didn't look down on the rest who preferred a more casual approach to fashion. Vanessa, in "air-conditioned" jeans gave new meaning to summertime grunge. With high school out for the summer, she could wear whatever struck her fancy—and almost anything did.

"I'm here, everyone!" Peggy Carson spilled into the room, whipping off the apron she wore as a waitress at The Cup & Saucer. Her quilting skills were improving rapidly, and everyone enjoyed her life-of-the-party spirit. Then, too, it was always entertaining to see what Peggy's beautician sister had done to her hair. Today, pink streaks had been woven in and out of her dark tresses.

Good-natured gossip and chatter prevailed as the women pulled out their projects. A Stitch in Time had flourished over three decades under the capable management of Mary Beth Brock, whose prowess with a needle was legendary. She ran a tight ship, too, which included the tutoring of Stony Point's needlewomen.

All eyes turned when Mary Beth suddenly pushed through the back-room door in navy blue slacks and a blouse accented with a burgundy smock. She pivoted on sturdy shoes and clasped the handles of a wicker basket big enough to obscure her portly frame.

"What on earth?" Stella Brickson intoned, dropping her knitting into her lap.

Vanessa leaped up to help, but Mary Beth had a firm hold on the basket, which Annie could see was covered with a cloth the size of a baby blanket.

A look of pride—or joy—or both beamed from Mary Beth's face as she approached the table with the basket. She looked flushed and almost young. Certainly she'd lost a good ten of her sixty years. "I've a little surprise for you!" she warbled. And Mary Beth, who had never been known to "warble" in her life, set the basket down. Gingerly she pulled the blanket back.

A mewling mass of multicolored kittens tumbled about in the basket, all furry tails and awkward paws. They blinked filmy blue eyes and emitted plaintive little cries from wide-open pink mouths. Everyone gawked at Mary Beth's surprise with little sighs of wonder.

"Vanessa and I found them last week—abandoned in

the window well, the one right over there on the south side of the shop." Mary Beth, who had never married, beamed like a new mother. "We've been taking care of them, feeding them from a bottle! Would you believe it?"

Kate crossed her arms over her green jacket and regarded Vanessa with a mix of concern and pride. Notoriously allergic to cats, she had obviously chosen to view the whole maternal scene from a safe distance. Ironically, and luckily for the kittens, her daughter, Vanessa, had recently started volunteering at the animal shelter.

"We had to give them Pedialyte just like they were human babies," Vanessa said importantly. She leaned over the basket protectively, her long dark hair draping her oval face. "They were so cold; the vet said they could easily dehydrate. We had to warm them up first before we could try to feed them. Feeding a chilled kitten can be fatal, you know."

Peggy drew a fluffy golden kitten from the basket and rubbed the small body against her face. "But where is the mother?"

Stella Brickson did not rise but craned her long neck to see the squirming feline mass. "There must be four of them. No. Five!"

"The mother's feral. She abandoned them," Mary Beth said matter-of-factly. "We're not sure how long they were left on their own, but they were pretty weak when we hauled them out. Poor little things. But so far so good. We only lost one. Just yesterday." At this last bit of information, her brown eyes grew soft.

The largest kitten had tufts of ginger and black fur in a ragged pattern. Its tiny face was gold but for a black patch over its left eye like a budding pirate. Two of the kittens were gray, and one had inherited color genes of every description. The fattest was gold with oddly crooked stripes on its tail and ears.

Alice stroked the fur of the little pirate. "Oh, Annie, aren't they the cutest things you ever saw? I'd love to have this one when it's big enough. Is it a boy or a girl?"

Mary Beth turned to Vanessa who blushed slightly and responded, "That one's a boy. See, you can tell by the ..."

"Never mind," said Kate. "We'll take your word for it."

You're not going to keep them all, are you, Mary Beth?" Alice asked, exploring the small tummy with a perplexed grin.

"No, that I can promise you. Another week or so, and I'll be looking for good homes for every one of them. But they'll still need a lot of care." Mary Beth tucked the blue blanket around the kittens, which had been carefully returned to the basket. Her fingers moved gently near a listless black kitten smaller than all the others. "Not sure Blackie here is going to make it. It's hard to get enough formula into her. Lord knows she needs it more than all of them, but she's too weak to fight for her supper."

"We should get them back by the stove," Vanessa said, taking hold of one end of the basket. "Miss Calloway showed me what to do."

Carla Calloway, a single woman in her fifties, had recently purchased the property known as South Shore and transformed it into a shelter. Stony Point gossip held that she had pretty much used up her considerable fortune to rescue abandoned animals of the region.

"In between shouting orders, no doubt," Kate said with a sardonic expression. "Carla Callous is lucky you haven't quit like the others. Nobody can take her critical tongue for long."

"Yeah," Vanessa said with a shrug. "But the animals are so cool—and she's good with them. You guys are still going to have the benefit show for the shelter, aren't you?" The teenager cast hopeful glances around the room of needlecrafters.

"We said we would," Mary Beth said staunchly.

"You'll get no thanks for it, mind you," Stella Brickson intoned with an unrestrained *hmph!* "She's as prickly as a riled porcupine."

Annie pondered Stella's remark and wondered what made Carla Calloway prefer the company of animals—if indeed that was true of the woman she had yet to meet. Personality aside, her care of Stony Point's abandoned animals had made a significant contribution to the community's well being. "She's providing a wonderful service. We have to applaud that," Annie offered diffidently.

Nods and sighs ensued, indicating willingness—however reluctant—to raise funds to augment the dwindling resources of the shelter's founder.

Annie looked down at the tiny black kitten, its head weakly snuggled in the soft blanket. The filmy eyes seemed to meet hers briefly, and then slowly close. "Poor little thing," she whispered. She felt a strange urge to pray for the tiny black runt with no mother.

At length, Mary Beth cleared her throat. "Well, then, we've had enough *Animal Planet* for today. Now, since we've committed ourselves to the benefit auction, we'd better not waste any more time."

But Annie smiled to see that Mary Beth could not resist one final fond look at the basket as Vanessa carried it through the door.

~ 2 ~

"Just get rid of all this junk now before the lease runs out—unless you want to pay another month's rent on your mom's place!" Jem Carson glowered as he spoke, his swarthy face close to hers in the weak lamplight. His dark eyes roamed the tiny apartment with quick, dismissive glances.

Tara wanted to tell him to go, but it was never smart to get Jem riled up. Besides, she was just so tired. "I will. I will. Just give me a minute. She was my mother, you know." She hadn't expected to feel any great sorrow upon learning of her mother's death. Now, tears gathered at the corners of her eyes and threatened to spill over.

Her mother had raised her in a series of tawdry apartments on Boston's lower east side. Tara remembered the day-care centers and later the public schools. She remembered her mother lying in the twin bed with the torn pink dust ruffle, too tired or sick or sad to fix breakfast. Later she would go to work and return with hamburgers or Chinese takeout, which they would eat in front of the ancient television set. By the time she was in high school, Tara knew her mother no longer worked. Each month she would open a long white envelope, and there would be money for groceries.

The turbulent teen years brought more misery, more mistakes. She'd left home at 16, deciding she wouldn't look back. There must be something better in life, and she would find it.

Tara pulled clothing from drawers, stuffing them in a box. She tried to pack things up without looking at them, to pretend none of it mattered. She didn't want to recall the sad lullabies, the fits of depression, the angry words, the tears, the longing. *Why is Mother so sad? Why doesn't she love me?*

Where had the years gone? She was nearing 30 years of age and had nothing to show for her life. No husband, no children, and since November, no job. She'd moved around New England in search of better-paying work, but with only a GED in place of a high school diploma, she was left with few options. And lately she'd found being on her feet for hours at a time exhausting.

Would she end up like her mother—dead at fifty of heart complications or too many pills? She shuddered and dumped a variety of bottles and magazines into a plastic tub.

She watched Jem plunk himself down in a faded armchair and switch on a football game on television. They'd met in Portland along the wharf where he'd been fishing. She liked to walk along the waterfront, to watch the boats bobbing in the water like brave little sailors ready to launch their next great adventure.

"I grew up in a place like this," he'd said, peering over her shoulder. And that afternoon he began to describe a little place farther north along the Maine coast where there were lighthouses and lobster boats, town socials, and picnics on green lawns. Buried inside that burly, wild exterior was someone sweet, almost tender.

Did he still love her? What lay between them now seemed little more than habit or convenience. Mostly, he just took off for weeks at a time on some new venture that he was sure would make him rich and never did.

Tara opened the drawer of her mother's scarred desk. The thin cushion covering the chair slipped as she scooted closer. Her mother had been raised in Boston by parents who boarded their only daughter at expensive schools in winter and shipped her off to relatives in summer. When her father died suddenly, leaving nothing but an astounding trail of debt, Tara's mother had lived a year with a widowed aunt before running away with an Australian sailor.

Tara couldn't remember the man who later became her father. He died three weeks before she was born—or so she was told. Her mother refused to talk about him and became eerily silent on the subject of her grandparents. Whoever these people in her mother's past were, they'd taken her mother with them—along with any hope for happiness or love in her short, sad life.

Tara swallowed hard. She felt bitterness well up like bile inside her. Life was a cruel joke played on the unsuspecting.

Tara's fingers traced broodingly over the little knobs on the desk drawer. She had been angry when she left home, determined to get something better out of life. But as time passed, her thoughts returned to those sketchy, difficult years, and the mother she had needed so much. If she had been a better child, would her mother have been happier? Would she have loved her?

She paused, arrested by the realization that during the last few years her mother had seemed more peaceful. Maybe she'd finally found relief in one of the many prescriptions that were supposed to relieve her depression.

"Get a move on!" Jem exclaimed. "I'm not hanging

around here much longer." He got up and walked a few angry paces toward her. Then, hearing the roar of some exciting play, he went back to the chair and the football game.

"All right! All right!" Tara frowned and let her eyes linger briefly on the man in the chair. He was still young, but his beautiful black hair was thinning. He hadn't shaved and had the beginnings of a paunch. He had seemed so dashing, so confident—her knight in shining armor riding a great black horse. (A white one would have been too much to hope for.) Life would be different, and she had embraced the sensation of being loved.

What did Jem see when he looked at her now? She raised her eyes to the filmy mirror on an adjacent wall of her mother's studio apartment. When had she grown so thin? The curly hair clouding her shoulders looked dull and lifeless, her eyes enormous. They were brown. She'd always wished they could be blue—blue as the ocean.

"I can see the world inside them." Jem had said that when they met along the waterfront—could it have been a year ago? The image in the mirror frightened her suddenly. She felt ugly and alone! As alone as her dead mother had been. What if Jem left her too, this time for good?

She tore her eyes away and pulled open the desk drawer. Just a few more things to go through. Trembling, she lifted a small packet of letters tied with a pink ribbon. Her mother had loved all shades of pink from shell to raspberry. Was this little bundle a sentimental record of some lost lover? Or could these be letters from the man who'd died before his little girl was born? Her eyes darted left and right; she felt like an intruder.

Dear Claire,

I'm so glad to hear from you after so many years. I am old now, but one does not forget the important things, or the people who have shared her life in some way.

You would love to see how spring has come to the bleak landscape around Grey Gables. Where once snow lay thick on the lawn and brittle branches streaked a dull sky, all is green and growing. The ocean has come to life again. The ice has broken up and is rushing away, chased by warm, westerly winds. Little green shoots and tiny flowers jump up everywhere. One can see that God, who is even older than I am, has not forgotten the important things either. In spite of our winter souls, he has sent spring once more.

I'm sorry you have not been well. You must take care of your health, and above all, remember that you are not forgotten.

It was handwritten on pale blue paper and dated April 4, 2009. The lines were straight, but the letters slightly wavy as though formed by an unsteady hand. The words sounded like poetry. She read down to the final line; it was signed, "Elizabeth Holden."

Who was Elizabeth Holden, and why had her mother written to her? Tara drew out another blue envelope, opened it and read a letter dated that same year but four months later:

Dear Claire,

I was sorry to read you have been ill and that things are not going well. You sounded very upset in your last letter. That grieves me very much. There are good facilities in Portland where you can get help, but I hope you know that you are welcome here at Grey Gables.

The rose bushes are glorious. New blooms appear every day, and I drink in their fragrance coming through the open windows. You would especially like the pink ones that grow along the path leading to the road. I gave my neighbor a great bouquet for a wedding party she was attending today.

I pray for you every day and for Tara. I'm sorry she cannot come more often to see you. Write to me soon and tell me all your news.

This one was signed, "Love, Elizabeth Holden." Tara stared at her name on the page. Whoever Elizabeth Holden was, she not only knew her mother but her as well. *I pray for you every day and for Tara.* Was this some relative her mother never talked about, even as she never spoke of her father or the grandparents Tara had never known? Tara read and reread the letter, the commiseration over a neglectful daughter. *I'm sorry she cannot come more often to see you.*

A wave of guilt swept over Tara. It had been wrong to stay away so long. She should have spent more than a few hours on Christmas day with the mother who, though she may not have loved her, had given her life. Claire Andrews had died alone, not having seen her daughter for months on end. No one had come to her aid, only a kindly woman who once knew her and hadn't forgotten—a woman who wrote letters about roses and ocean breezes and had been gracious enough to invite her mother into her home—an idyllic sounding place … Grey Gables.

Tara rifled through more letters, each similar in tone, containing uplifting thoughts, expressing concern, giving assurances of prayer, along with little asides about the life of an elderly woman in a house where ocean breezes wafted through the windows ... . *I can still see well enough to work my needle. I hope you like this cushion cover I made for you. I stitched one like this for my daughter many years ago; perhaps it will remind you of your own child.* And the signature ... Love.

Tara looked down. The cushion had slipped off the chair and fallen to the threadbare carpet. She stared at the beautifully worked design that featured a cradle near an open window. No face could be seen, but inside it a baby must be asleep. On a table next to the cradle, pink roses flourished in a crystal vase. Filmy wind-swept curtains revealed a cobalt blue ocean on which a distant white sail glinted beneath a summer sky.

She imagined her mother holding that cushion and looking into the cradle. Did she see small curved lips and wide trusting eyes beneath a cap of curly hair? She swallowed. Did she think of her? What had she done to so disappoint her mother? What could she have done to make her mother love her? Well, it hardly mattered now.

Jem pulled himself out of the chair and strode over to her. "Pack it up, and let's get out of here!" He released a long disgusted sigh. "What are you doing now?"

His words were slurred, and she realized that he was slightly drunk. He'd had a couple of beers in the car on the way and another while he watched the football game. "It's these letters my mother saved," Tara stammered, drawing her shoulders in. It was a reflex whenever Jem had been drinking. He was as likely to give her a shove as a kiss, especially when he got impatient. "And this pillow. It's beautiful, and it's got initials in the corner. See, E.H—Elizabeth Holden ... like the signature on these letters."

"Lot of sentimental claptrap." He grabbed the pillow from her hand and seemed about to fling it across the room. Suddenly he stopped. "Hey! Wait a minute. I know that name."

He snapped the letter from her hand. Knitting dark brows together, he studied it first, and then the handworked cushion. "Yeah. That's the old lady from Stony Point! Well, can you beat that? Imagine your mother knowing Mrs. Holden, the grand lady of Grey Gables."

He grabbed up the little stack of letters and the cushion, and strode back to the easy chair. He chewed the inside of his cheek as he poured over the letters with the cushion on his lap. He began stroking his left jaw, a gesture that meant he was planning something, and *that* meant trouble.

She got up, pushed a carton to the front door with the side of her foot, wishing she hadn't come. And yet, she was glad she'd seen the letters—there was comfort in them. Her mother had died alone in a stuffy apartment, but she had known the hand of love in her final years ... even if it was just an old woman, miles away. Elizabeth Holden had known her and had not forgotten. *I pray for you ... and for Tara.*

"Yeah, it just might work," Jem was mumbling, more to himself than to her. "This could be just the luck I need." He continued to rub his long, stubbly jaw as he refolded the letters. "Here, tie these back up and find something to put this pillow in. And be careful with it."

Tara felt a chill in spite of the airless heat in her mother's apartment. She tucked her arms into her old blue sweater. "Jem, what are you talking about?"

"It's J.C.! I've told you a million times. Not 'Jem' or that ridiculous 'Jeremiah.' Can't you get it right?" He put his fist down on the arm of the chair, bobbing his head in frustration. A strand of black hair fell over his forehead. "Jeremiah Carson was a dumb kid cutting traps on the dock, falling over his big stupid feet while his puny brother followed him around like a lost puppy dog."

"Whatever," she said, letting go a long sigh. Pretentious initials aside, he was still the overgrown little boy with grand ideas that never came to anything. Ah, she knew how to pick them.

"Hold onto your hat, Tara my girl. We're going back to Stony Point. When those snooty townsfolk ticked me off, I said I wouldn't go back ..." He gave her a rare kiss on her forehead and looked down at the handworked pillow. "Now there's something in that old backwater town that just might be worth the trip."

Perhaps the place held some good memories for him. A place where pink roses bloomed, and where one could look out on the ocean. Her mother had seen such a world.

"People in these parts are dying to buy up Mrs. Holden's needlework. I saw one in the Brown Library the other day— and a big write-up about the artist. And to think I knew her as a kid. Me and Wally used to do stuff for her at that big house on Ocean Drive."

Tara dropped down on the couch across from him. Jem was talking about picking up and leaving again. She was desperately tired. "Je ..." She caught herself. "J.C., you know I haven't been feeling well lately. I can't ..."

"Country air is just what you need!" he said. He didn't look at her. He was seeing something beyond the room. His eyes gleamed with that frightening, yet magnetic shining he got when he was excited.

"I don't understand ..."

"There could be a fortune in that old house. And your mother was a friend of the lady who owned it. You read it ... that sweet stuff about being welcome and all." His lips curled in a confident smile. "I hear her granddaughter lives there now—a widow who inherited the place from Mrs. Holden. And you're going to show up at Grey Gables."

"I'm *not!*" Tara crossed her arms over her chest.

He ignored her protest and pushed out his lower lip in a thoughtful gesture. "We're going to that little Maine backwater burg, but you're going to show up alone. You won't know me. You're just a girl alone who's learned her mother has died; you have no place to go and no one to turn to. You just want to meet the lady who comforted your mother in her last years."

"And then what?" Tara demanded wearily. "What good is that going to do?"

"Just leave it to me." He stroked his jaw in concentration. "We'll go slow. We have to be real careful. Now, grab that junk. We're getting out of here; I've got some thinking to do." He got up, cradling the pillow and letters in his big hands.

Tara followed, shivering in her thin jeans and sweater. Her arms full of cartons and bags, she didn't even close the door behind them. The landlord would come and throw the remaining pieces of her mother's life in the trash bin. Poor Claire Andrews. All that was left of her was one skinny failure of a daughter who hadn't even said goodbye.

— 3 —

*I*t was late when Annie said goodbye to Alice. They'd gone out to lunch at a vintage tea room and had taken their time coming home. It had become their practice to make Tuesdays special, beginning with the Hook and Needle Club meeting; today had been no exception. They stopped at several roadside vegetable stands, found some luscious-looking strawberries, Granny Smith apples, and sweet corn with variegated yellow and white kernels. Their arms were bulging when they finally decided to call it a day.

After seeing Alice off, Annie dined late on frosted wheat cereal for supper. She answered her email, spruced up the kitchen, and took the sweet corn out to the porch. The messy task of shucking was best done outside where the wind or plucky birds could take the silky hairs stripped from the ears. Boots followed with a look of intrigue on her whiskered face, but Annie expected little help from the feline quarter.

The sun hung low, melting into bands of gold and dusky rose. Strips of charcoal clouds rose as though chased upward by some unseen hand. That subtle light, as day began to die, evoked a certain sadness; something precious was coming to an end. While there was hope for tomorrow, this day would never come again.

She had often witnessed day's end with her husband,

Wayne. The spectacular Texas sunsets they had shared were so explosive with color and movement that it seemed you could almost hear them—like pyrotechnics on the Fourth of July. It always brought a lump to her throat, and she would squeeze his hand, knowing that he was hearing the fireworks too. Here at Stony Point, sunsets were no less lovely, but quieter—like music. Each night the melody was unique. Sometimes it was vibrant and chaotic; other times, it was methodical and tranquil.

Today, the music was slow and haunting, and Annie felt a peculiar melancholia. There was no one to turn to, to point to the sunset and say, "How lovely!" And in a sudden flash she thought about Ian, the venerable mayor of Stony Point, who had quickly become her friend. There had never been more than friendship between them; she'd made sure of that, in spite of hints that his feelings lay deeper. Still, it would be nice if he were here right now. She'd fix him a glass of that strawberry lemonade he was fond of, and they could just talk ... *Ah, Annie,* she rebuked herself. *You're just feeling lonely. It will pass.*

She leaned back in Gram's wicker chair and ran her fingers along a smooth green ear of corn. She let a long green strip fall and watched Boots bat it with tentative white paws. The cat sniffed it and tossed her head in spontaneous play.

"It's just you and me, Miss Boots," she said softly to the swish-swish accompaniment of cornhusks across the porch floor.

She glanced up, suddenly aware of another sound. It was coming from far off, like sudden wind through beach grass. But the night air was still; no wind disturbed the leafy overhang of trees. The sound stopped briefly, and then started up again. Was someone walking up the overgrown path that led to Grey Gables? Annie often took that shortcut after a walk along the water, but visitors usually used the driveway.

Annie dropped the corn into a green bag and walked toward the path lined with daylilies and daisies. Perhaps Alice had forgotten something or was coming back for a chat. "Hello?" she called, a little nervously. Stony Point neighbors seldom locked their doors, even at the height of the season when tourists abounded. It was charming, even though it might be foolhardy. Hadn't she learned anything after that pirate cove map had been stolen and the incident with the greedy antiques dealer?

She called again, but there was no answering voice. Perhaps a tourist had taken a wrong turn. Suddenly someone appeared at the top of the path—a girl—or a woman markedly thin in a cotton sundress dragging a duffle bag too large for her small frame. A mass of hair gave her head a too-large-for-her body look. Dark curls fell over her eyes, and then suddenly, it was the girl herself falling.

Annie ran toward her, reaching her just as she righted herself into a sitting position. The girl lowered her head onto her knees and wrapped her arms around them. Goose bumps rose all over her exposed flesh. Annie dropped down beside her. "Are you all right?" She clutched one arm, and felt its clammy chill.

The girl raised her head and peered up from red-rimmed eyes, her face pale. "I'm sorry, I ..." She put a hand to her head and swayed slightly, as though the negligible breeze unbalanced her. "I didn't mean to intrude." Her voice was small and raspy, as though it hadn't been used in a long time. She tugged awkwardly at her skirt, trying to smooth it over her knees. "I felt a little faint. I ..."

Why was this stranger climbing up a private path? Should she call for help? The silence stretched as Annie tried to work out what to do. Had she fainted again? She removed her sweater and wrapped it around the girl's shaking shoulders.

"Oh, thanks," she said, sitting up straighter and meeting Annie's eyes. "I'll be OK. I'm really sorry. I—saw your light and ... well, my car broke down outside of town, and I just started walking ..." She broke off, dropped her gaze from Annie's and reached for the handle of her bag.

Annie saw now that her surprise guest was not a girl, despite her willowy form. She had to be somewhere in her late twenties or early thirties, and she had the look of someone whose life had not been easy. Small lines around her mouth seemed the more prominent in a face too thin to be pretty. Yet the velvety eyes had a classic nut-brown beauty above a straight nose.

"Can you walk to the house?" Annie asked. "My name's Annie Dawson, and I live just up there." She pointed toward Grey Gables. "It's not far." She helped the girl to her feet, feeling the trifling weight against her as she rose. "You probably could use a cup of hot tea."

"Yes, thank you," she stammered. "I'm really sorry to impose ..." She said nothing more but walked unsteadily, leaning on Annie's arm.

Annie dropped the girl's bulky nylon bag in the hall and led her to the living room. Settling her on the sofa, she wrapped a pink and green afghan around her shivering guest's shoulders. "Do you want to lie down?"

"No, thank you. You're very kind, but I'll be fine." She ran the tip of her tongue over dry lips and drew in a series of shuddering breaths. Gradually she became calmer. "My name's Tara. I'm from Portland, and I ... well, I ..." She broke off and a shadow passed over the brown gaze.

"Well, Tara from Portland, you just rest. I'm going to put the kettle on," Annie said, patting her arm. Tara was not a child, but everything about her begged consolation. Boots had scooted in behind Annie and sat looking on with her usual calculating yellow gaze. "She won't bother you, but she does like to hop onto the couch to gain access to the window."

"She's beautiful," Tara said, a ghost of a smile touching the bow-shaped lips. "I—like cats." But she made no move toward Boots. Instead she leaned her head back against the sofa and closed her eyes.

When Annie returned with the tea and a plate of open-faced sandwiches, Tara appeared not to have moved an inch. Her eyes flickered open, and she sat upright. "Oh, this is very kind of you."

"Do you take anything in your tea, Miss ... ?" Had she mentioned a last name? And was she a "miss"?

"It's Frasier. Tara Frasier."

"I'm pleased to meet you." Annie handed her a delicately flowered cup of Earl Grey tea. She could see that Tara Frasier wore no rings. Her nails were short and somewhat ragged, as though she hadn't cared for them in some time. Still they were well-shaped, sensitive-looking hands. They trembled slightly when she took the cup.

"Are you sure you don't need to see a doctor? I could drive you to …"

"No, please. I … I really am all right." She took a sip of tea and glanced around the room as though she were looking for something.

"Your bag is in the hallway, Tara." Perhaps she had medicine in it, which might account for why she hadn't left the heavy thing in the car when she set out on foot.

"Oh. Thank you." She took a small pimento cheese sandwich from the tray that Annie held toward her. "I guess I *am* a little hungry."

Annie sat in a chair across from her and set her own teacup on the tray table. Boots quickly leaped upon her now unencumbered lap, and Annie stroked her soft fur. It was quiet in the living room except for the steady ticking of the mantel clock. Annie had never known it to be so loud before. What had brought Tara Frasier to her door? Why had she simply left her car without calling a tow truck or arranged for a ride to a hotel or something?

"Tara, do you want me to phone someone for you?"

"No. There's no one. I …" She broke off and set her cup down on the coffee table in front of her. She let the afghan fall around her and folded her hands nervously in her lap. "My cellphone died, and I realized I didn't have my charger cable with me." She pushed a swirl of misplaced hair back with her index finger and clasped her hands together once more. "You see, I …" Once again she let the sentence drift into space. Her wide brown eyes filled.

"Never mind," Annie said gently. "We can deal with it in the morning. You can stay here tonight. There's plenty of room." Aghast, Annie listened to the words coming out of her own mouth. This woman could be anyone! A thief ... an axe murderer! What was she saying?

A small sob escaped Tara's lips. She nodded her head back and forth as though in dissent or dismay. Annie couldn't tell which, but she found herself reaching across the space between them to cover the small clasped hands. "Whatever it is ..."

"I'm really sorry. I'm not usually so emotional. It's just that my mother ..." She paused, ringed her lips with her tongue once more, and fixed her eyes somewhere over Annie's head. "My mother just died. She—she's been ill, really, for some time, and I ..." The words fell away again in another half sob.

"Oh my dear," Annie said, struck by the girl's vulnerability. "I'm so sorry." Indeed, Annie did know, for she had lost both mother and father. She was still working through the two latest losses in her life—her beloved Wayne and Gram. Darkness crept around the windows of Grey Gables. She pulled a clean tissue from her pocket and gave it to Tara. A lamp on an automatic timer breached the encroaching night.

"I just had to get away. I didn't know where to go, or what to do. I just got in my car and drove up the coast." Tara dabbed at her eyes. The skirt of her pale blue sundress was torn near the hem, perhaps from climbing up the rugged path from the road; a green stain smeared the bodice. "I—I should have known my old car wasn't up to another road trip. I've been meaning to trade it in, but I lost my job, and then Mother ..."

Annie patted Tara's clasped hands and remained silent. It was no wonder she was a bit disoriented after what she'd been through. In a broken economy, a lost job was not unique, but for each person it happened to, it was a new and wrenching story. Then to lose someone important to you was a double sorrow.

"My car broke down in Petersgrove; then I took a bus. I didn't have enough cash to go farther than Stony Point, so I just started walking. Then, when I saw your light ..." Tara didn't finish the sentence. "You've been so kind, and I really don't want to impose. Is there a hotel or a bed and breakfast nearby?"

Annie drew in her breath, pursed her lips. Was she serious? From the look of her, she couldn't afford a cheap room—even with a credit card. And it was clear that her health was anything but robust. She shook her head slowly from side to side but gave Tara an encouraging smile. "There's no need for that. It's late, and you've been through a lot. I have a perfectly good bedroom upstairs. I used to sleep there when I visited Grey Gables as a child. You see, I've only come to live here recently, after my grandmother passed away."

The brown eyes widened with something like curiosity or camaraderie. "It's a beautiful house. When I saw it from the road, it was so grand and inviting. I thought it might even be a bed and breakfast." She paused; the eyes softened. "I'm sorry about your grandma. I had one too ... Well, everyone does, don't they?" Her lips formed a self-deprecating smile. "But I—never knew mine."

"Well, mine would tan my hide if I let you go off to a

motel. So it's settled." Annie got up and pushed the tea service off to one side. She held out a hand. "Come on now. You need your rest. In the morning, we can talk some more."

Tara rose and paused briefly before taking a step, as though to test her ability to move. Perhaps she *was* ill. Was it wise not to insist on calling a doctor or seeking out a clinic? But she was well over 21—certainly old enough to be responsible for her own health. Still, the drawn, white face concerned Annie. "Good thing you have your bag with you." She hefted the yellow nylon duffle. "Let me bring it up for you." Its weight surprised her; it probably weighed as much as the girl herself.

Annie opened the bedroom door, freshly painted in cool almond. Wally had done himself proud. The interior walls were painted a muted coral; the color provided the perfect backdrop for the Betsy Original depicting a portion of Grey Gables's patio—a white wicker chair and pots of colorful geraniums clustered around it. At the windows were lightweight accordion blinds and filmy valances of white with green ivy trim. Coral and sage accent pillows dotted the matching coverlet.

Annie bent to place the duffle bag on a rack she'd found at a garage sale and had painted white. She had bought canvas strips in a lovely floral pattern, and Wally had secured them with his staple gun. "You'll find an extra blanket in the closet," Annie said, rising. Her guest stood transfixed, as though not knowing what to say. "It's small, but you should be comfortable here. The bathroom is just across the hall. There are plenty of towels and such in the linen closet."

Tara's eyes widened. Her gaze was fixed on the

cross-stitched wall hanging. "My grandmother was a needlework artist," Annie explained. "This is one of her early pieces."

"Oh, it's so *beautiful*," Tara said. She stood just inside the doorway, one hand resting on the mahogany bookcase that still held Annie's favorite childhood books—*Black Beauty, Wind in the Willows, Anne of Avonlea*. The horse-head lamp with its garland of daisies cast a subtle glow from beneath its crisp new shade.

"Well, you should get some rest. We can talk in the morning. I'm just down the hall—to the left—if you need anything."

"Yes," Tara said, her eyes still riveted on the cross-stitch. "Thank you."

Annie closed the door. Boots had come up the stairs with them and now followed Annie down with a little murmuring half-meow. "What?" she asked. "I just did what your former mistress would have done in my place." She reached down and stroked the cat from head to tail in one swift motion.

Actually, Gram had taken in many visitors. As she cleared away the tea things in the kitchen, Annie wondered if taking in strangers was the wisest thing to do these days. She picked up the cordless telephone and dialed the familiar number.

"It's me," Annie said into the phone.

"What's up?" From the sound of it, Alice was putting dishes away with the phone cradled against her shoulder.

"I have a visitor," Annie said. "I just thought I should tell someone, since I don't have a clue who she is."

Silence. Even the tinkling of crystal stopped.

"She just showed up at Grey Gables with a duffle bag,

and believe me, she was in no shape to move on. She practically fainted at the top of the hill. Says her car broke down in Petersgrove. Then she took the bus as far as Stony Point and started walking."

"You mean, you're putting her up overnight?" Alice asked with mild incredulity. "Why didn't she walk to a motel?"

"She thought Grey Gables might be a bed and breakfast. At any rate, she's worn out, and from what I can gather, she has no money. Her name's Tara Frasier, and she's from Portland." Annie paused, aware how strange this all sounded—indeed how strange it really was. "She's a grown woman, but she's pretty upset. Her mother just passed away. Anyway, she needs help. I—I just wanted you to know ..."

"You mean, in case you're murdered in your sleep? Honestly, Annie, you're such a pushover." The clatter of dishes ensued.

"Come over tomorrow, and I'll introduce you," Annie said. She hung up with a smile. She wasn't afraid, but it was good to know Alice was nearby. She was glad that her best friend had not reminded her of the time the stranger who'd filled in for Wally turned out to be a jewel thief. She switched off the kitchen light and went upstairs, curiously lighthearted.

No one could say her life was dull.

— 4 —

*T*ara Frasier woke with a start—disoriented. She squinted into the sunlight that penetrated the window blinds. It was a strange room ... soft almond walls, muted coral accents, and valances trimmed with green ivy. Directly in front of her hung the finely cross-stitched canvas of a sun-spattered patio with a white wicker chair and red geraniums. The blue ocean, dotted with white caps, stretched endlessly in the background. It was beautiful, haunting, strange.

And then she remembered. She fell back against the soft sheets so delicately fragrant that she suddenly wanted to cry. She'd been taken in, given shelter in this lovely place, and warmed with tea and kindness.

"She's just one of those rich widows with more money than sense." Jem's rich baritone, made flat with derision, echoed in her mind. "Probably never had to worry a day in her life like the rest of us. Well, maybe it's time she spread a little of it around."

"But, Jem ..." she had protested.

"I told you, it's J.C.! Jem Carson was that dumb kid cutting traps on the dock. I'm not that kid any more. You and me ... together we're going places. You and me, honey ..."

Then he had buried his head in her shoulder, her curly plume of hair a cushion between them. And her heart had swelled with tenderness. Poor Jem. Nothing seemed to work out for him, no matter how hard he tried. His mother had died when he was a child; his father's death allowed him and his brother, Wally, to run amok. They'd had to grow up quickly, to fight their way into a world that gave them little welcome. Wally had married Peggy, and the responsibilities of marriage and fatherhood had smoothed his rough edges. Jem was still just rough.

"You're the best thing that ever happened to me," he had told Tara more than once. He had said other things too, but that was the drink talking. The angry bullish man he sometimes became wasn't really who he was. Jem was sweet and strong, and he loved her. *Didn't he?*

Her head felt fuzzy. She pillowed deeper into the soft fabric of the bedclothes and wished Jem were with her now. But they were not to be seen together. No one must know they knew each other.

"But couldn't we meet sometime?" she had asked him.

"Listen, honey," he had interrupted. "It's got to be this way. You have to make that lady trust you so you can help me. She's got plenty of those fancy pictures hidden up there. What's one or two? For us, baby."

Tara sat up on the edge of the bed, tucked her feet into the soft plush rug, and felt a wave of dizziness come over her. She had to be strong; she had to think. Surely today, Annie Dawson would want to take her to Petersgrove to recover her disabled car—the car that didn't exist. She'd be eager to get rid of her unwelcome houseguest. Tara sighed. What was she going to do?

She rose gingerly, taking a deep breath of the scented air. The window had been left open just enough to usher in the ocean breeze. It smelled heavenly. Pink and white roses blooming beneath the window added a luxurious fragrance. She felt like Alice in some sort of wonderland that wasn't altogether new. She had been here in some long-ago dream never quite forgotten.

I pray for you every day and for Tara. The woman named Elizabeth Holden had known about her as well as her mother. She had invited her mother to come here. Had she ever come? And if she had, why would she choose to leave?

Tara looked out on the idyllic view. The ocean shimmered beneath a radiant, blue sky. Reluctantly, she let the blind fall back in place. Her future here was nothing if not bleak and unpromising. Why was she allowing herself such foolish flights of mind? She could hear Annie moving about downstairs, perhaps wondering what her guest was up to. She'd have to get up, face her brief benefactress and explain herself. How long had she slept?

She fumbled through her bag for a clean pair of jeans. Steadying herself on the edge of the dresser, she wriggled into a clean jersey shirt. How could she possibly keep up this charade? What would she tell Annie? Jem had dropped her off as close to Grey Gables as he dared, and she had walked the rest of the way and climbed up the hill. There was no broken-down car. But that she had felt ill and breathless when she arrived was very much the truth. What was making her so tired these days? Had the old anemia returned? Would she have to take those big red iron pills again? She hated pills, recalling the bottles lined up on her mother's scarred dresser.

A soft scratching at the door broke in on her thoughts. She opened it to find Boots looking at her with a quizzical expression on her gray, whiskery face. The cat waited de-murely, as though to ask why she was still in bed on a glori-ous summer day. Tara had no idea of the time, but the sun had begun its climb into the blue reaches of sky.

She sprayed her hair to calm the wild curls and secured her headband over it. She applied some quick blush to her cheeks and descended the carpeted stairs. She forced her-self to remain calm, but her heart was beating a wild tattoo in her chest as she approached the kitchen.

Her hostess was dressed in blue jeans and a white polo shirt over which a denim apron had been hastily secured. Blonde hair with silvery traces gleamed in the light from a bay window. A boy and a girl of kindergarten age grinned from photos on the refrigerator door. Pictures obviously drawn by their small hands clustered around the photos. On the coun-ter and table, vases of flowers shed bright splashes of color. The woman's movements were vibrant and energetic. Hardly the picture of the rich, spoiled widow Jem had drawn.

"Good morning, Tara," Annie said as she pulled a tray of delicious-smelling muffins from the oven rack. She dropped an oven mitt on the table and extended a hand. "Please sit down. I have coffee—or tea, if you prefer it. I hope you slept well."

Tara swallowed, clasping her hands to keep them from trembling. "I—I did sleep well, Mrs. Dawson. I ..."

"It's Annie. Just Annie, and I'm glad you slept well, but truthfully, you still look a bit peaked." She studied Tara's face.

Tara looked away, anxious lest Annie Dawson see be-neath the pale skin and the dark-ringed eyes directly into her heart. She straightened her shoulders and smiled.

"I'm much better ... thanks to you."

"So, will it be coffee or tea?" Annie asked. "Now, Miss Boots, keep out from under my feet," she quipped to the cat circling her ankles. She placed two muffins on delicately painted blue plates.

"Tea, if it's not too much trouble," she replied, taking the offered chair and savoring the aroma of the muffins.

She was surprised to realize she was actually hungry. For days she'd had little or no appetite. Maybe she *was* getting better. The dizziness would pass; she'd feel more like her old self. Jem had tickled her protruding ribs the last time he'd held her in his arms. He'd frowned and told her she was getting as skinny as a cadaver. She shuddered at the grim comparison.

Annie handed her a cup of the same blue china in which last night's tea had been served. She sat down across from her. "Welcome to Grey Gables. It's a lovely day," she said with a smile.

Tara was grateful not to be riddled with questions as they ate companionably in the brightly lit kitchen. The white tablecloth, edged with red and lime green accents, was set with matching place mats and napkins. Boots had jumped up onto the window ledge and sat sunning herself, occasionally licking delicate white paws.

Tara longed to remain in that tranquil space without speaking, but she had to say something to explain herself. Last night she'd been too tired, too ill; but Annie Dawson would want to know who she was and what her plans were. She would surely be anxious to see the back of the troublesome guest who had been thrust upon her.

She tried her best smile. "Mrs. ... uh ... Annie," she

corrected herself. "I want to thank you for letting me stay last night. I'm much improved this morning, and after this delicious breakfast, I feel even better. I'll just get on my way and ..." She let the words fall away because she had no idea what to say next. Her pulse began to race.

"Tara," Annie began matter-of-factly. She moved her plate and cup to one side and leaned forward, slender hands folded on the table. "There's no hurry. You just enjoy your breakfast. When you feel rested enough, I'll take you to Petersgrove to see about your car. Likely, it's been towed into town by now and ..."

"There is no car," Tara stated, looking directly at Annie. She twined her fingers together in her lap and looked away. She bit her lower lip. After a few seconds of silence she repeated, "There's no car. I hitchhiked. You see, I lost my job. I couldn't make the payments on my car. Then my mother got sick. When she died, I didn't know what to do."

Annie's face registered surprise, but something more—gentleness, concern. Tara looked down again, amazed at how easily the lies came. Oh, it was true enough she'd lost her job, and she had no car, but she hadn't gone to Portland to care for her ill mother. She'd come to dispose of her things and seal up the apartment in which she had died—alone.

"I'm so sorry," Annie breathed. "But hitchhiking! That's so dangerous. Wasn't there someone you could call? A sister or an aunt or someone?"

Tara shook her head. "I don't have any family. There was just my mother and me. I was married, but we were divorced after only a few years, and we never had kids." It was perhaps the only thing she was grateful for and the only thing that saddened her—often to the point of tears.

God, if there is one, must have known that I couldn't have cared for a child, she thought. The needle-worked pillow with the cradle surrounded by pink roses in a crystal vase pushed its way into her mind.

"I'm sorry," Annie said gently. A little furrow between her green eyes deepened. "But sometimes friends can be as close as family. What about *your* friends, Tara?"

She gave a little laugh and hoped she didn't sound as bitter as she felt. She had casual acquaintances at work, companions to have a good time with for an evening, but there was no one to really talk to—no one but Jem. And lately that had been less than comforting.

"Your job, Tara. What did you do before you were let go?"

Had Annie thought a career kept her too busy for friends or family? The truth was she'd had a lot of jobs—waitressing, retail sales, whatever she could find. She'd never gone to college; she'd drifted from one entry level job to another. The best job was her most recent, but you could hardly call working for Wolverine Sign Incorporated a career.

She'd done service banners, truck lettering—all sorts of interior and exterior signs. She had been one of several workers they'd had to let go when the recession hit. *Last hired, first fired*, she thought. She couldn't blame them. Besides, she'd called in sick too many times in recent weeks. Tara licked her dry lips, knowing Annie was waiting for an answer to her question. "I worked for a sign company—I did some hand lettering, and I set the machines for styles and designs. Routine work mostly, but I'm pretty good with computers. I don't have any formal training though."

Annie lifted the delicate cup to her lips and drank. "I'm sorry it didn't work out."

Tara sipped from her own china cup, glad for a pause in the conversation. She was supposed to make friends with the lady of Grey Gables and secure her trust. She knew she was making a bad start, but she had no idea how to proceed. Jem would be furious.

"So you hitchhiked to Stony Point." It was a statement more than a question, and Annie appeared to mull that idea around in her mind.

A woman looking for work would have stayed in Portland or traveled to Boston or some large city, but she had moved down the coast, and ended up in a small town. Tara knew it was hardly believable. "I guess it wasn't the best idea, but I just had to get away after mother ..." She let the sentence drop, lowering her head.

Annie rose to switch on the electric teakettle. She paused at the window seat to stroke Boots's silken fur and no doubt to ponder how she might gracefully tell her house-guest it was time to move on. That she hadn't yet done so surprised Tara. In fact, it amazed her that she, a stranger of no apparent means, had been given shelter in the first place.

In the space of seconds an idea unfolded in Tara's mind. "I'm—grateful for your kindness, but I have to tell you something. I didn't just happen to come here. I came on purpose."

The atmosphere was suddenly charged. Her hostess returned to the table. She sat down and looked at Tara, her expression registering confusion.

"I came to Grey Gables because of a letter I found in my mother's things. Actually, there were several letters over the last five or six years. They were from Elizabeth Holden of this address." Tara hurried on, hoping her story was believable. Well, this part was true, at least. "It was obvious that my mother had spent some time in Stony Point and that Mrs. Holden was a friend. I just wanted to find her and thank her for being so kind to my mother. I didn't say anything last night because ... well, you weren't her. And then you told me she had passed away, and I realized that I wouldn't be able to thank her."

Annie's eyes widened; the light sprinkling of freckles stood out on her nose. She had to be shocked by this revelation and angry at being lied to.

Tara raced on: "I should have told you this right away. I'm sorry I made up the story about my car. I thought if you knew I was a hitchhiker you wouldn't help me. I was really tired. Lately, I've not been feeling very well. I hope you'll forgive me ..." She looked down at her hands, waited for Mrs. Annie Dawson of Grey Gables to politely ask her to leave.

The silence stretched out. It could all be over in an instant. She saw everything falling apart—Jem's plans, her place in his heart when he learned of her botched efforts. This time he might leave her for good. And something in the back of her mind teased at an even greater loss. Well, she'd lost her self-respect long ago, hadn't she?

"Tell me about your mother." The words fell softly between them.

Tara looked up, expecting to see anger—or at least censure—in her hostess's green gaze. She blinked, breathing deeply to stop the whirling in her head. "Her name was Claire Andrews. She was ..."

What could she say of the mother she knew so little about, who had withheld her secrets along with her love? Something like hunger pain churned inside Tara. She toyed with a muffin crumb on her napkin.

"She used to come here when she was a girl. She knew your grandmother. The truth is, we didn't get along very well when I was growing up." Tara paused. "I left home when I was sixteen. It was a mistake, I know that now. Funny, how you're so sure of things and then ..." A wave of dizziness swept over her.

Annie rose and came around to her chair. Tara felt a warm hand on her shoulder, and heard the quiet voice. "Perhaps you'll show me those letters. I'd like very much to see them. But right now, I think you need more rest. Why don't you go back upstairs and lie down while I clear up the breakfast dishes."

Tara rose, allowing Annie to steady her. "I—I shouldn't impose any longer, Mrs. Dawson," she began weakly.

"It's *Annie*, and you are not imposing. Now, go along and do as I say." She spoke gently but guided Tara to the steps with a firm hand. "When you feel better, bring the letters out to the porch. I'll be working on a crochet project for the animal shelter. We'll soak up the sunshine." She paused and then added with emphasis. "And we'll talk then."

Back in her bedroom, Tara lay on the soft white coverlet and wondered what would happen next. Perhaps it was the weariness washing over her that made her want to cry, or it might have been the unexpected kindness from a stranger who had no idea what she was getting into.

~5~

ally Carson steered his boat toward the dock,
enjoying as always the feel of sun on his back and
the wind in his hair. His peapod had a shallow draft and
maneuvered like a dream. He'd only had an hour after
finishing up a project for Stella Brickson, and time had
passed too quickly. It always did when he was fishing.

He and his brother, Jeremiah, had spent much of their
youth on their father's sixteen-foot Swampscott dory. Wally
knew that if he hadn't become so good with wood and tools,
he might well have become a lobsterman—like his father.
But unlike his father, he'd found that peace and significance
came from something more powerful, more profound.

He was lucky to live in this place that he'd loved all his
life, and he was lucky to have work to do. And besides, he
had a family of his own now. He and Peggy, a waitress at
The Cup & Saucer, had made a good life for themselves.
They had waited a long time for Emily, but she was worth
every anxious moment of the wait. Wally felt himself smiling. That morning she'd flung her six-year-old arms around
his neck and begged for a story.

"Tonight, Miss Twinkletoes!" he had chided. "Our stories are for bedtime. Today, you've got things to do—and so
do I."

Emily loved his stories—mostly made-up tales about a

ballet dancer who got into all sorts of adventures but continued to wow audiences with her graceful art. Madeline had to be in the stories too. The cloth doll Emily loved had a mop of yellow hair, a pink tutu and ballerina slippers that crisscrossed up her stuffed ankles.

Between Peggy's tips at The Cup & Saucer and his handyman jobs, they'd been able to get lessons for Emily at Myra's School of Dance. A recital was coming up, if memory served Wally right.

"You ready?" Peggy had come streaming into the front room of their cottage, clutching her apron and purse. Her short hair was hastily moussed; her vivid blue eyes sparked with light. "My customers will be waiting!" She grabbed Emily by the hand.

Their summertime routine included taking Peggy to The Cup & Saucer and Emily to day camp. As a handyman, Wally could work at his own pace, freeing him to cope with all their schedules. They had only the one vehicle, a slightly feeble pickup truck with more speed than dignity, but it got them where they needed to go.

The hour on the water had flown, but it had restored his peace. Peggy would be expecting him for supper soon. He pulled the peapod into the trawler bay that belonged to Todd Butler, who operated the town's best fleet of lobster boats. The summer Wally had broken his arm, Todd had hired him to do odd jobs while he healed and now let him tie up at his docks whenever he wanted to. Todd's brother, Ian—Stony Point's ubiquitous mayor—had put a good word in for him. Ian Butler looked out for Stony Point citizens.

Wally smiled. Soon he would be working at Grey Gables

again. Annie Dawson had told him she wanted her pantry refurbished to match the cabinets he'd recently done. He loved helping Annie restore the old Victorian house she had inherited from her grandmother. Yes, he was a lucky man to have a place here with neighbors who cared.

Reluctantly, he tied up his peapod, left the wharf and headed down the beach. It was a spectacular Maine afternoon. The sand was warm beneath his feet, and a soft breeze cooled his face. The tourist season was in full swing, but most people had left the beach area and had gone in search of supper. Wally liked this time of day when a man could be alone with his thoughts. It was quiet and peaceful as he walked toward town.

"Hey mister, can you spare a dime?"

He hadn't heard anyone behind him. The out-of-the-past cliché was odd, but there was something familiar about the question—as familiar as the voice, rich and deep with a slight twang. Wally whirled around.

The man behind him was sturdily built, well-tailored clothing belying any need for a handout. He was wearing sharply pressed slacks and a pale blue shirt under a nicely cut jacket. The worn loafers he wore fell a bit short of the overall well-groomed look; maybe he just preferred the comfort of old shoes. He was older and heavier, his dark hair tinged with silver, but the ironic grin and laughing eyes had not changed.

"Jem?" he croaked, grabbing the extended hand with both of his. "Is that really you, man?"

"It's me, but call me J.C. More sophisticated for a man in my position, eh?"

Wally swallowed hard, trying to take in the changes in his brother. He hadn't seen him in quite a while. As kids they'd run along this beach and swam like two dark fish until their lungs were bursting. *Mister, can you spare a dime?* They'd used that line with tourists when they wanted money for soda or snacks. These days a dime wouldn't buy a soda straw or a candy wrapper.

Then the stormy teen years had come, and they'd been in more than their share of trouble. Wally's mind whirled with memories. He'd been no saint then, to be sure, but Jem had a special knack for getting in harm's way. Folks said the two of them had been the death of Pop.

There had been no feminine hand to gentle their rough edges. Their mother had died of cancer when Wally was ten. Dad's downward spiral had begun then. Most days he came home from fishing in his old boat and drank until he passed out in the living room chair. Wally and Jem were pretty much left to their own not-so-wise devices.

Peggy had saved Wally from total destruction, but for Jem there had been no savior. It was rumored that he liked the drink too, and that he liked loose women, but most of all, that he liked money. He'd always been a schemer, sure his next idea would make him rich. Wally remembered how Jem had devised a plan to swipe buoys after dark and exchange them with their own so they could haul in a bigger catch the next day.

Jem slung an arm around Wally's shoulder as they walked, turning away from the beach and taking Grand Avenue toward the downtown area. They were nearing the town center, but Wally paused and turned to Jem ... or was it J.C.?

The last he'd heard, Jem had dabbled rather unsuccessfully in an import/export business and lost his shirt. Obviously, he'd found a new one—a rather nice silk one that fit snugly over his expanding waist. But he was still a handsome man. It had been years since he'd seen Jem. Wally wondered why he never came around.

Jem always said he was an outsider, the black sheep. "Besides, I ain't gonna be no smelly lobsterman; I've got better fish that need frying!" Wally remembered him saying that. Jem, it seemed, had little interest in his roots. Last year's Christmas card had arrived in March like the afterthought it probably was. And Wally never had an address to send his brother one.

Given the train wreck of his teen years, maybe it was a good thing Jem hadn't hung around Stony Point. Wally kicked at a tuft of crabgrass hedging the walkway. But you'd think when a guy had family he'd show up once in a blue moon. Well, here he was, right beside him, tall and muscular. Jem had always made Wally feel small.

Wally thought about what Jem had said. *A more sophisticated name for a man in his position?* "So what *position* do you have now?" Wally asked hesitantly.

"Well, little brother, I'm a businessman—real estate— Boston right now." He clapped Wally's shoulder, gave it a proprietary shove, and looked him up and down. "And you're looking pretty good yourself." He glanced down at Wally's boots. "You lobstering like our old man?" He said it with good humor, but in the old days Jem had little good to say about the man who'd raised him.

Wally shrugged and gave his head a little shake. "Now

and then, when I'm not building or repairing something, I hire on with Todd Butler's crew. Got my own boat; Todd lets me tie up at his place." His boat was a simple peapod, but he'd bought it with his own money, and she was a tight little craft. He said nothing about searching the bay for birds; Jem would likely consider that a sissy thing to do.

"Old Todd made good for himself," Jem said tersely, "but having your brother as the mayor can't hurt."

For having been away so long, Jem had a remarkable memory for names and events. Wally stuffed his hands in the pockets of his jeans and felt his balled-up fists, a sign of the old tension he used to feel around Jem. Wally always craved his respect, but at the same time he distrusted him. He looked up and saw the sun glinting on Jem's black hair that still dipped over his left eyebrow. "Been a long time," he said.

"You still work for the old lady who owns that big Victorian house on Ocean Drive?"

"Mrs. Holden passed away; her granddaughter owns it now." He paused. "So what brings you to Stony Point?"

Jem stopped, drew in a long breath, and looked back toward the lighthouse, the marina and the bay, golden with molten sunshine. "Yeah," he said in a dreamy exhalation, "it has been a while, but the old place looks the same. Maybe a bit more prosperous. Lobstering and tourism ain't been half bad, seems like." As they gazed over the well-trimmed lawns, the neat shops, the clean boardwalks, and the busy beaches, Wally felt pride in his hometown.

"We do all right," Wally said. "Summer people spread the word; seems like we get more every year." He waited for an answer to his question. Why had Jem turned up now?

"I tell you, little brother," Jem began with a slow drawl. "Real estate's in a bit of a slump right now, so I thought it would be a good time to get a little R and R. And why not good old Stony Point? Catch up with my kin." Jem rubbed his jaw. "Is the Shark's Head still around? I sure could use a drink."

Wally hadn't touched a drop since he and Peggy had gotten married. But not staying sober had a lot to do with the accident that put him in Stony Point General for six weeks where he'd had time to think about where his life was going. Reverend Wallace had told him God was watching out for him and that there was a reason for everything. Wouldn't Jem get a good laugh out of that! Church and God were topics for old ladies, he'd say, not for real men.

"I gotta get home," Wally said uncomfortably. He moved on toward his truck parked in the shade along Cedar Street. He had retrieved it after Peggy had finished her shift. "Peggy will be waiting supper." He fished for his keys with fingers still stiff from balling his fists. He wasn't about to have a drink with Jem or anybody. In the old days they had sometimes swiped bottles from his dad's stash—but those were the old days.

"So you're married now, little brother?"

Wally winced over the "little brother" bit. You'd think they were still kids instead of grown men in their thirties. "Best thing I ever did. We have a little girl; name's Emily." Jem would remember Peggy from high school since she lived next door, but Peggy never asked about him. There were a lot of the old locals who would remember Jeremiah Carson, certainly. "And what about you, Jem? You have a family?"

"Me?" Jem quipped, as though the idea were outrageous. "Nah, I've had a few close calls, but no girl has tied me down yet."

He'd had his choice of Stony Point girls, Wally remembered, and Jem had liked to party. But you'd think by the time a man reached his age that he would settle down. "My place is just there, beyond that rise. Come on. Peggy will put on an extra plate."

"You sure, man? I hate to intrude."

"You've been gone a long time, but you're still family, Jem." And Wally was surprised to feel a lump form in his throat.

"Maybe you wouldn't mind introducing me as J.C.? There are folks around here who'd just as soon forget Jeremiah, if you know what I mean. I'd hate to get off on the wrong foot with the good folk of Stony Point."

Wally shrugged and opened the door to his cottage. "Come on in. It's not the Ritz, but it's paid for, and Peggy's fixed it up real fine." Wally stood aside, waiting for Jem to pass through. A glance around brought a quick sense of relief. Peggy must have gotten home from The Cup & Saucer early enough to tidy up. On Wednesdays a co-worker gave her a ride home, picking up Emily on their way.

"Daddy!" Emily flung herself at him, her hands clutching his legs. "You smell like fish!" She wrinkled her tiny nose, and seeing Jem, cocked her blond head to one side.

"This is Je—'er—J.C.," Wally said, "my brother—and your uncle. He's come for a visit." Wally felt a burst of pride. He'd always yearned for Jem's approval, sulked when it never came, and finally had simply let it all go. He no longer needed it; he never even talked about Jem anymore, not even to Peggy. But suddenly, the old feelings crept up from somewhere. Truth was he'd never stopped caring, even when Jem had been, for all intents and purposes, kicked out of town. Not that there hadn't been reasons. What had brought him back? Was all that talk about position and success true or was Jem still looking for that dime?

"Hello, Mr. J.C.," Emily said with her usual friendliness, cocking her head to one side and peering up at him.

"Well, Miss Emily," Jem said, taking her hand and kissing it like she was a princess or something, "I'm very pleased to meet you!"

Emily stared out of curious blue eyes, her mouth quickly forming a smile.

"Can this be the same girl I knew in high school?" Jem extolled as Peggy appeared at the kitchen door. "You don't look a day older!"

Peggy had changed into jeans and a soft lavender sweater that was one of Wally's favorites. Her cheeks were pink with pleasure at the compliment. Jem was being too bold, but then Wally was always protective of his Peggy. She said something about wishing she'd known they were having company; she'd have cooked something better, but soon they were situated around the table.

"I hope you like meatloaf," Peggy said, unfolding her napkin. "Did I miss you at our wedding? And what does J.C. stand for? When we were kids, it was always Jem!" Peggy could rattle on and ask more questions at one time than anyone Wally had ever met. He studied Jem's swarthy face.

If he was going to go around calling himself J.C., people were going to ask.

"I love meatloaf," he said, "and I flog myself for missing your wedding, my fair lady. Alas, I was out of the country at the time. As to your third question ... Jeremiah Hamilton Carson at your service."

Wally groaned. Jem could be such a ham! All that high-toned speech!

But Peggy was clearly charmed. Wally felt a fleeting stab of envy—well, maybe just concern. Peggy was always ready to embrace the world, accepting everyone at his word. Innocence had its price, though, and he worried about her.

"God is great, God is good ..."

Emily, eyes closed and hands folded, had begun grace before the meal as she always did. Wally glanced at Jem whose fork was poised in midair ready to attack the meatloaf. He narrowed his eyes like he was surprised or embarrassed. Wherever Jem had been in the last 15 years, he wasn't used to praying. They hadn't been raised to think about a God who deserved their worship. Sundays had been for fishing and hanging out.

Jem recovered from the prayer and began talking about places he'd visited. Every now and then he'd throw in a compliment for Peggy or a wink for Emily.

"So, where are you staying while you're in town?" Peggy asked while they ate pineapple upside-down cake for dessert.

"Actually, I'm staying over in Petersgrove."

An odd choice, since Stony Point was by far the more attractive resort town in the area. But Wally wasn't surprised that the town's bad boy wouldn't want to get too up close and personal. Still, it had been a long time, and few would really remember him. At least not the way he looked now. Besides, lots of kids sowed wild oats.

"If you don't mind," Jem said, as though he had read Wally's thoughts, "I'd prefer putting some space between myself and the good citizens of Stony Point. That is ..." He cleared his throat and said with a shrug, "... best if they don't know the black sheep of the family is cooling his heels in these parts."

Peggy frowned. That could be a tough call for his friendly wife, Wally knew. She liked to share the town gossip, but she'd be careful since that's what Jem wanted. "Well, don't be a stranger," she said, that bloom in her cheeks rising again. Clearly, Jem had captivated her. "You're welcome to come by for dinner anytime." She glanced at Wally, her eyes bright, expecting him to second her invitation.

Wally wiped his mouth with his napkin. "Sure," he said. Jem had been seventeen when he left Stony Point, and Wally was fourteen. They had gone to live with their grandmother when Pop died. Standing on her porch, he'd watched his brother climb into a glued-together rattletrap Ford and take off with a wave of his hand. "So long, bro." And that was when Wally knew that fourteen-year-olds could weep.

"I won't get in your way. I know you two are busy, but I wouldn't mind a look around the old place ... The Cup & Saucer, Butler's Lighthouse, Grey Gables ..."

Wally looked up. Peggy had rambled endlessly about The Cup & Saucer, but he had mentioned Grey Gables only in passing. Jem had asked about "that Victorian house on Ocean Avenue," which was surprising enough, but he even knew its name. Maybe his brother remembered more about his old roots than anyone thought.

But Wally realized that his hands had once more balled into fists inside his pockets.

— 6 —

Annie sat on the porch with her crochet project and a pot of Earl Gray tea. It was late Wednesday afternoon, the day after Tara had shown up at Grey Gables. Alice was on her way. She would have been on Annie's doorstep that morning if she had not had an important Divine Décor party that kept her busy all day. Annie put up a hand in greeting as Alice came up the walk. "About time," she called.

"I came as soon as I could," Alice said, collapsing on a wicker chair next to Annie. She peered into her face. "What? No black eye? No blunt-force trauma?"

"I'm perfectly fine. And keep your voice down."Annie poured a cup of tea for Alice. "Tara's resting upstairs."

"Tara. Now there's an earthy name. Who is she, and why is your houseguest in bed at this time of day. It's nearly supper time!"

"The girl's been through a lot, and I don't think she's well."

Alice uncovered a foil-wrapped plate to reveal half a dozen muffins with a heavenly aroma. "Cherry cheesecake," she chirped. "Tell all and I'll share!"

"Ten pounds a whiff!" Annie mourned. She sighed and thought for a moment before replying. The "all" she knew about Tara Frasier wasn't much, and explaining it was likely to be difficult. "Well, she recently lost her job. And her mother died. The poor girl doesn't know what to do."

Alice pushed up the sleeves of her green-and-pink plaid shirt, and her silver bracelets tinkled musically. "But how did she happen to show up here at Grey Gables?"

Annie took a few contemplative stitches in the doggy jacket she was making. Mary Beth, owner and champion of A Stitch in Time, had suggested that since they were launching a benefit for the local animal shelter, handmade pet products would be just the ticket. The single crocheted pet coat Annie had chosen hardly required close scrutiny; she could use the time spent on the undemanding pattern to sort out her thoughts. "Well, at first, she told me she just stumbled upon Grey Gables after her car broke down. But actually, she didn't have a car, and she came here on purpose."

"You're harboring a prevaricator?"

Annie drew in her breath and let it out slowly. "I don't think she lied exactly. Apparently she found some letters that Gram had written to her mother who just died. She said she had come to thank her, but then when she realized Gram was gone …"

Alice's frown deepened. "Why didn't she say so in the first place?"

"She came here right after her mother's death and was pretty upset and confused. Actually, she nearly collapsed on the climb up to the house. She was in pretty bad shape. She thought that I wouldn't help her if I knew she had hitchhiked all the way from Portland."

"Hitchhiked?" Alice parroted. "All the way from Portland?"

Annie shrugged, and prepared herself for Alice's chiding. *You're such a pushover, Annie, especially when there's a mystery afoot.*

Alice made the charge only with her eyes. Looking sidelong at Annie, she said, "What do you think is wrong with her?"

"I don't know. She was real unsteady on her feet—especially last night. And she was pale as chalk. I think I'd better take her to the clinic."

"Annie, what are you saying? She's not your responsibility."

Annie studied the stitches in her crochet project and waited. She didn't want to sound all pious about being a brother's (or a sister's) keeper. But surely a young woman who lands on your doorstep and needs you ...

"I mean, she could be anyone," Alice said more quietly. "She could be—"

"She has no job and no family. She's all alone. I think Gram would want me to help her; she seems so lost."

Alice sighed. She took a muffin from the plate and held one out to Annie. They munched silently for a few seconds before the sound of the screen door halted their reverie. Tara stood on the threshold, paling at the sight of Annie's guest.

She took a step back to retreat into the house. "I'm sorry. I didn't know you had company."

"Alice isn't company. She's my best friend from next door. Come on out and have a cup of tea and one of her homemade muffins. Fair warning. They'll probably spoil our dinner!" Annie gestured toward an empty wicker chair at the table. "No one makes muffins better than Alice. Alice MacFarlane ... Tara Frasier."

Tara took the chair Annie had indicated. Her wild crop of curls had been tamed with a headband, and she wore a pink top under an oversized white shirt. She held out a thin hand and met Alice's gaze briefly before dropping her eyes. "Hello," she said softly. She took a muffin and watched the steam rise from her cup of tea. Her eyes roamed over the ocean and sky and the flowers blooming in a riot of color. "It's so beautiful," she said wistfully.

"Did your mother visit here, Tara?" Annie asked after a few moments of silence while the three of them gazed into the distance appreciatively.

"I—I think so, only I don't know for sure. She didn't talk much about herself, and I left home when I was pretty young."

Annie and Alice listened to Tara's account of an unhappy childhood, of loneliness, and of her struggle to make ends meet on a meager income. Tara didn't know anything about her father other than the name he'd given them. She told them she herself had once been married, but that the union had ended unhappily. "My mother and I were never close. I always wanted to be ..." She broke off and caught her lower lip in her teeth. "I didn't realize how sick she was. I'm afraid I wasn't there for her when she—" Her chin trembled, and tears began to fall quietly down her cheeks.

Wordlessly, Annie pulled a tissue from her tote bag. Tara dabbed her eyes and blew her nose, and then played with the tissue in her lap before speaking again. "I really need to know about my mother. You see ..." She looked out over the bay, suddenly earnest. "I wasn't there for my mother. I think in some ways I felt she hadn't been there for me, and

I was angry. But there was someone who helped her—your grandmother, Mrs. Dawson."

Annie nodded, then said softly, "Please, Tara, call me Annie."

Tara pulled something from the pocket of her jacket. A packet of letters tied with a pink ribbon. She untied the ribbon, and pressing out the folds, handed a letter to Annie.

Annie read silently, her fingers tracing the pale blue stationary along the familiar handwriting. The letter was dated April 4, 2009. She read the flowing lines that conveyed Gram's poetic expression. Gram wrote that she was glad to hear from Claire "after all this time." Following was an artful description of Stony Point, the blossoming of spring, and the ocean view from Grey Gables. She ended by urging Claire to take care of herself and assuring her that she wasn't forgotten.

Annie's eyes blurred when she read her grandmother's name at the end of the letter. It was so like Gram to reach out to people who were lonely or ill. It sounded as though Tara's mother had been both. Claire Andrews, the mother of this fragile young woman, had once been right here at Grey Gables, perhaps on the very porch where they were sitting.

"How did your mother know Mrs. Holden?" Alice asked, leaning forward in her chair.

"I don't know." Tara frowned. She looked off toward the ocean and was quiet for a long moment. "I have another letter," she said then and handed Annie a second sheet of the pale blue linen stationery. Annie scanned the letter and began to read out loud, hoping she could keep her voice steady:

Dear Claire:

I was sorry to read you have been ill… That grieves me very much. She skipped over more news about Stony Point, a description of summer roses, and an invitation to Grey Gables. Softly, she read the final lines: *I pray for you every day and for Tara. … Write to me soon and tell me all your news.*

This time the signature read "Love, Elizabeth Holden." Annie folded the letter, and swallowing hard, gave it back to Tara.

"I found these letters after she died," Tara said. "I was clearing out the apartment and …" She broke off, near tears once more, and then in a rush of words said, "You can see why I needed to come here. I really want to know about my mother, to talk to someone who knew her, to … . Oh, I know it won't make up for the years. She's gone, and I never told her …"

Annie poured tea into Alice's cup and refilled her own. She saw that Tara's had not been touched. She cleared her throat, feeling desperately sorry for the young woman and wanting to defuse her anguish. "It's not unusual to feel guilty after someone dies, Tara. Perhaps your mother knew how you felt …"

"No, I don't think she did, and that's what really gets to me." Tara sounded a bit stronger, or perhaps self-recrimination gave an edge to her voice. "But I want to know her, you know? I want to understand …" But once again she broke off.

"My grandmother knew a lot of people, Tara. She was especially kind to young people and tried to help where she could. She was just that kind of lady. But *I* didn't know your mother. Perhaps she met Gram when she was very young herself; it could have been a long time ago. I've never come across any letters from your mother, though Gram never threw anything away. Still, there may be some folks in Stony Point you could talk to."

"She could come to the Hook and Needle Club meeting next week!" Alice interrupted. "I bet someone in the group knew her mother." She had directed her words to Annie but looked back and forth from one face to another. Obviously, Alice had changed her mind about harboring a liar and fearing for her best friend's life. But clearly she hadn't been thinking about Stony Point's reluctance to welcome strangers in their midst. Still, they were a fair bunch, and they cared about people, even "outsiders."

Annie nodded and said somewhat gravely, "That's certainly possible. You see, Tara, the Hook and Needle Club is for women who do needlework. We meet at A Stitch in Time, a store that sells supplies and provides instruction in all sorts of needlecrafts. You'd be welcome to come with Alice and me to our next meeting. It won't be until next Tuesday, but you'll need a few days to rest and get your bearings."

Tara looked from Annie to Alice with a mix of hope and disbelief. She shook her head of kinky curls and said, "I'm very grateful. But you've done so much, Mrs. ... Annie." She corrected herself.

Annie nodded. "And you can just stay with me for a while."

"I—I don't want to intrude. The lease on my apartment in Portland is good for the year, but I'd like to stay in Stony Point a little while, or long enough to find out what I can about my mother. I'd like to work, though, if I can find a temporary job. At least part-time."

Annie studied her, wondering at Tara's compulsion to learn about her mother's connection to Stony Point. Perhaps the girl had some resources, but was she strong enough to work, even if there was anything available? The only ad she'd seen in *The Point* was for someone to assist Carla Calloway at the animal shelter—again. The turnover was pretty frequent. No surprise there, given Carla's disposition. Even Vanessa, who loved being with the animals, steered clear of Carla when she could.

"You could check the paper to see if anyone's hiring right now," Annie suggested, "but you haven't been feeling well. Perhaps you ought to see a doctor."

"I was treated for anemia a year or so ago; it could be related to that." Tara seemed to consider her own diagnosis, and little lines appeared in her forehead. "I think it's just that I'm overtired, but I'll see someone; I don't think my health insurance has expired yet."

"I'll be happy to give you a ride into town," Annie said.

Suddenly there was a heavy thud, the sound of something hitting the ground.

"Is Wally working out back?" Alice asked.

A swooshing sound followed, as though something had fallen into the bushes. Annie got up, dropping the crocheted pet coat. Alice and Tara followed her around the porch where huge hydrangeas bloomed in pink and purple abundance. They walked to the rear of the house, scanning the area for anything unexpected. But they saw nothing to account for the noise.

"A deer looking for food, perhaps," Annie said. Or maybe it was a raccoon, though they usually prowled at night with their beady, ringed eyes. Beyond the yard lay a virtual forest, lush with pines and a variety of deciduous trees. She felt her pulse quicken and a memory returned as she surveyed the woods. She had once hidden in them—she and Amy, Mary Beth's niece, when Dorian Jones—also known as a jewel thief—had been chasing them.

"Oh, look here!" Alice said.

Annie turned to see Alice bending over a big pot of geraniums, one of several that lined the wraparound porch at the rear of Grey Gables. The pot was broken and soil lumped on the ground amid broken stems of bright red flowers. Boots suddenly hopped down from the porch and sat on the grass, curling her tail around her in her best innocent pose.

"Boots!" Annie intoned. As they rushed toward her, the cat leaped away into the hydrangeas.

Boots was nothing if not curious, and she could get into things. Once she'd unraveled an entire ball of tweedy yarn that took hours to restore, but she had never knocked one of those heavy pots off the porch rail. She was notoriously light on her feet. She might be guilty, but it was more likely that a deer or small animal that had caused the ruckus.

Alice began extracting flower stems from the soil and broken clay, her Divine Décor bracelets jingling. "Don't bother now, Alice. I'll get it later." Annie took Tara's hand to direct her back to the porch and was surprised to find it sweaty and cold. Her face was drained of color, and her eyes wide with fright. "It's nothing, Tara. Come on, the tea will be getting cold."

She was certainly a high-strung young woman to be unnerved by such a small thing, Annie thought. But then she was in a strange place among people she didn't know. But as they walked back to the front porch, Annie saw Tara glance over her shoulder, her lips set in a pale line. High-strung indeed.

— 7 —

Tara surveyed the tools Annie had provided for cleaning the wicker furniture: A paintbrush with stiff bristles that had been cut down halfway, a dowel with a sharp point, and a toothbrush. Tara had never cleaned wicker before, but she was eager to do something to show her gratitude. Annie had been so kind in the six days since she'd come, looking after her, providing rest and nourishing food, and arranging for a visit to the doctor. She wanted to do something in return. Something to make up for the lies—and for what she was going to do!

"Let me help," she had pleaded when Annie left to go to town. "I'm feeling so much better. I think those iron pills your doctor prescribed for me are already working. I'm—really grateful for your kindness."

Annie was wearing white jeans and a lime green top with a scallop of tiny white flowers at the neckline. Her blonde hair shone in the sunlight as she stooped to retrieve her crochet project and tuck it into her tote bag. She and Alice had errands to do that morning, she had explained. She would come back for her later, and they would go to the club meeting together.

Tiny gold flecks danced in Annie's striking green eyes. "Are you sure you don't mind doing this? I need to prepare the way for you to join us at A Stitch in Time. You see, people in Stony Point are wonderful, but they don't take to outsiders very well unless they've been warned that someone new is coming. I'll be back in a couple of hours—the meeting is at eleven o'clock—then I'll introduce you to my Hook and Needle Club friends."

"Of course, I understand. And I'm happy to clean the wicker," Tara said. Annie was actually going to leave her alone at Grey Gables—with free reign of the house and silverware!

"You won't get all the furniture done this morning. Just leave everything where it is when you need to change for the meeting. We can finish it later. Remember not to get it too wet, and once you've washed it, you need to dry it." She motioned to a basket in the corner that held clean white rags. "I've prepared a solution of water and ammonia. Once you dust, you can wash the furniture with the brushes. The toothbrush is good to get in small places, and the paintbrush can be used for the larger areas. The pointed stick comes in handy for those tiny grooves that trap the dirt."

Then Annie had climbed inside Alice's Mustang and left her on the porch at Grey Gables. Boots, who had followed her mistress to the car, returned and trotted lightly up the steps. The cat wrapped herself around Tara's ankles and purred a welcome.

"You too!" she scolded lightly, and stooped to stroke the velvety gray fur. Why did everyone have to be so kind to her? It made what she was planning to do so hard! She switched on the handheld vacuum to dust an overturned chair. Plying the nozzle into the most deeply soiled areas, she began to scrub. If only she could wash away the grime that had a choke hold on her heart.

It wasn't a total lie, she rationalized. She really did want to talk to someone who knew her mother; but the other part—the plan to steal valuable artwork—was Jem's idea. Maybe she could get him to change his mind or just be happy with one canvas. Then they could both get away from here and start over somewhere.

A shadow flashed across her peripheral vision, and suddenly a figure rounded the porch and came up the steps. "Jem! What on earth are you doing here!" She dropped the vacuum hose. "Someone will see you!"

"No one will be coming by right now," he said, panting with the effort of the climb. "But just to be sure, let's step inside."

"Jem, please! Annie could come back any minute. If she finds you here …"

He pushed her forward into the entry hall of Grey Gables. "They won't be back any minute. They just left. And no one is around except that neighbor of Mrs. Dawson's, and she drove off with the boss lady. So you see, we're completely alone!"

Tara closed the door and leaned against it, her heart beating a frightened rhythm. "It was you!" she gasped. "The other day when the flowerpot fell off the rail. You've been watching! Spying on us!"

"Blasted cat nearly scared me to death. When I jumped out of its way, my elbow knocked the pot over. Good thing the woods were so close."

"Oh, Jem. I hate this! I hate what we're doing …"

"Tara, sweet Tara," he said, coming close to her, "I've been watching, and you were terrific. The way you made the lady of the house fall all over herself to help you. You did just fine; you're a real actress." He wrapped his arms around her and nuzzled her head against his chest.

The familiar scent of him, all fresh and piney, and the warm breath of his mouth next to her ear made her dizzy. Why did everything just fly out of her head whenever he was around? "I missed you, Jem," she murmured.

"And *J.C.* missed you too, baby," he said. "So tell me, what have you seen inside that attic?" His eyes gleamed with hope and too familiar avarice.

"Nothing! I've only had a few days here. I can't just up and ask to look through her attic!" She caught her lip between her teeth and struggled to explain. "Besides, she's been ... so good to me. Can't we just forget about doing that? We could leave today ..."

She felt his body stiffen. He gave her a little push backward. He planted both hands against the door on either side of her and looked into her eyes. A strand of black hair fell lower on his forehead. He was quiet for a few seconds, but she could see a muscle working in his jaw, which meant he was angry. Then the little boy angst took over, that plaintive needing in him that always cut through her defenses.

"I need you to help me—to help us!" he whined. "I thought we were a team. You know how tough things have been for me. I need you, baby."

When he began stroking her hair, her arms and shoulders, she let her breath out in a long stream. "Jem ..." He silenced her with a kiss, and then drew back with a smile that made her wilt.

"That's my girl. Take all the time you need. I won't hurry you " He paused and added, "too much!" He rolled his eyes around the foyer and the view of Grey Gables's living room. "This is some place, and that picture!" He stepped toward the large cross-stitch hanging over the sofa in its gold filigreed frame.

The vibrant red-orange poppies seemed alive in the room, the verdant greenery giving the flowers sharp dimension. An intricate border design around the work drew all the elements together in splendid artistry. *A work of love*, Annie had said with such tenderness in her eyes.

"She's got stacks of pictures like that hidden away in that attic, I'll bet."

"Jem, you have to get out of here! What if she comes back and finds you here? Besides, I'm supposed to be cleaning the wicker on the porch."

"She's got you doing her dirty work already? Those rich ones are all alike. They don't want to get their hands dirty."

Annie didn't put on airs. And Grey Gables was no mansion—it was beautiful but modest. Why couldn't Jem understand? "That's not fair!" Tara retorted. "She's not like that."

"Yeah, yeah," he said wearily. He paused and raised his eyebrows as though a new thought had come to him. "She's got my brother, Wally, working for her too." He rubbed his jaw in that way Tara knew so well. "I must say, Wally's got himself a nice little wife, though. That Peggy, she's a real looker, rounded in all the right places."

Tara cringed. She hated it when Jem teased her about other girls. They weren't married, but they had an understanding, didn't they? She supposed he fooled around like many men did, but he always came back to her, didn't he? She was glad that Peggy—whoever she was—was married and hoped she wouldn't be bowled over by his charm.

"Well, sweet Cinderella, I'm going now. You can get back to your chores, but don't wait too long. I'll be watching." He slipped out the door and scuttled around the porch to retreat from Grey Gables the back way.

Tara knew she'd lost valuable time, but she managed to completely clean and dry one chair before flying up to the guest bedroom to change into something presentable for the club meeting. She imagined it was some kind of quilting bee attended by a bunch of dried-up old women with time on their hands. But Annie Dawson was nothing like that; nor was Alice MacFarlane with her shining hair and glittering rings.

She had barely changed out of her work clothes when Annie and Alice returned to pick her up. She tucked in her blouse with nervous fingers and smoothed her hair. She could choke Jem for waltzing in on her, getting her all upset and nervous. She forced a cheerful smile as she got into Alice's Mustang. Then they were off for the quilting bee.

Actually, only one quilt was in evidence when Tara arrived at A Stitch in Time, and the women of varying ages and dress were anything but dried up. Glancing around the tidy shop with its colorful banks of yarn, fabric, and threads lifted her spirits. The cheerful ambience in the room took the edge off her newcomer anxiety.

"This is Tara Frasier, a friend who's staying at Grey Gables for a while," Annie said, introducing her. "She's come especially to visit with us and to meet people who might have known her mother."

A sturdy woman of sixty or so, wearing a maroon smock and a gentle smile, took both of Tara's hands in hers. "I'm Mary Beth Brock, the owner of A Stitch in Time. Welcome to the Hook and Needle Club." Her eyes were kind but shrewd; no doubt the owner of a thriving needlecraft shop had to be astute in business, Tara thought. She'd have to watch her step around this one.

She was introduced to Kate Stevens, a woman in her late thirties. When Mary Beth referred to her as "my right-hand and left-hand girl, without whom I'd be handless," Kate's laugh was quick and light. "Her daughter Vanessa is still in high school," Mary Beth continued. "Vanessa won't be here today; she's volunteering at the animal shelter, and the boss wouldn't release her today."

At the sound of a disapproving "Hmmph! Her boss is right!" Mary Beth turned to a tall octogenarian with upswept gray hair whose knitting needles fairly sparked with friction. "And this is Stella Brickson. Mind you, Mrs. Brickson's a charter member and a walking encyclopedia on Stony Point lore!"

Tara shivered at the sight of the straight-laced elderly woman with eyes that seemed to bore right through her. But she relaxed a little when the hint of a smile appeared and the white head bent slightly in her direction. A walking encyclopedia. Had she known her mother?

"And I'm Gwendolyn Palmer. But you may call me Gwen like everyone else." The lady wore a gorgeous silk blouse and a purple paisley scarf caught at her regal neck with a glittering brooch. She was knitting something fluffy and lavender. Definitely a woman of style. Suddenly Tara felt dumpy in her jeans and peasant blouse.

A tinkling bell announced an arrival, and Tara glanced up to see a young woman with short dark hair whip off a pink apron. "I'm sorry I'm late. Every tourist in Stony Point has visited The Cup & Saucer today." She flashed a wave to everyone around the circle, and Tara could see that her nails were painted purple. They'd go well with Gwen Palmer's scarf!

"Don't worry about it, Peggy. As long as you get here, we're all happy," Annie said. "And how is Wally, my favorite handyman? I can't wait to get him back to have a go at my pantry shelves."

Tara flinched. So this was Peggy. And she was part of this group! Tara tried not to stare at the glossy hair and the well-endowed figure. Someone was introducing her, but she couldn't focus on what was said as she watched the energetic waitress mould herself into an easy chair and kick off her shoes.

"Nice to meet you, Tara," Peggy said as she pulled a partially completed quilt of pink and green squares from her tote bag.

Mary Beth linked an arm through Tara's and said to the gathered women, "I'm going to show our guest where the coffee supplies are. Carry on. We won't be long. Then we have some business to discuss."

"Oh!" Tara breathed when they reached the back of the shop. "They're adorable!" A basket of kittens was tucked into an alcove. A palette of variable color and design, they squirmed and mewled in a fluffy tangle. A tiny black kitten lay rather still but gave her an inquisitive glance before dropping its head like a dark stone. She dearly loved animals. As a child she'd always wanted a pet, but her mother had staunchly refused.

"Their mother gave birth to them in our window well," Mary Beth said. "Vanessa and I have been taking care of them since their mother abandoned them. And they're doing pretty well. Even poor little Blackie there."

Tara longed to pick it up and cuddle it, but it was so fragile. Suppose she dropped it? She felt a pang in her chest like a long-forgotten memory suddenly sharpened. How often had she sat on the faded plaid couch waiting for her mother to wake up? It was a loneliness that continued into adulthood. Yes, she knew what abandonment was.

"It's all right. You can touch them. They're too small to bite." Mary Beth had taken her momentary pause as fear.

And perhaps it was, but it wasn't fear of the kittens. Instead, it fear of abandonment, of loneliness, of life. And she was frozen on the spot until she heard the sound of coffee being poured into a ceramic mug.

"It's ironic, really, since we had just decided to run a benefit show for the local animal shelter," Mary Beth said. "It's not an official shelter or anything, at least not yet. Carla is just a citizen who takes in animals. Some of these little guys might end up there if we can't find good homes for them." Mary Beth handed her the mug.

She took a sip, finding it mellow and sweet with an almond flavor. "Thank you. This is nice—very nice." She clutched the coffee self-consciously.

"Annie tells me that you used to work for a sign company."

Mary Beth cocked her head to one side and raised an eyebrow.

"Yes, it was mostly signs and such, and I do enjoy drawing." Tara felt herself relaxing a little. She was glad for this short reprieve. One stranger at a time was better than a whole cadre of them at once.

As though she had read her mind, Mary Beth said gently, "Now, Tara, when we go back out there, everyone will be working on a project of some kind. Maybe you could sketch out a few ideas for our animal shelter benefit. I'll give you all the pertinent information, and your hands can be just as busy as all those hands out there. What do you think?"

"Sure," Tara said, warming to this woman who seemed to understand her awkwardness.

"And you'll gradually feel free to talk. Believe me, they may appear daunting, but they're pussy cats. All of them."

Mary Beth placed her near Annie, Alice and Kate. Tara began reading the information Mary Beth had given her.

"Did you see the kittens?" Kate asked, eyes gleaming.

"Yes. They're so cute. Especially the tiny black one," Tara agreed.

"If the mother cat could see them, I bet she'd be sorry she'd abandoned them, don't you think?" asked Kate.

Annie cleared her throat, and frowning at Kate, said, "The mother could very easily have been injured or caught by some predator. Maybe she *couldn't* care for her young. It happens, you know." She glanced across the circle. "Stella knows that Stony Point has its share of wild animals. She was raised here and knows this part of Maine forward and backward."

"I believe what she means is that I'm old as dirt," the venerable aged woman said, but without bitterness. A smile leaked from her eyes. "What Annie says is true, but it's useless to speculate. We all know Mary Beth will turn over every rock in Stony Point to find homes for those kittens."

"Stella and my grandmother were good friends when they were young," Annie explained to Tara, giving Stella a fond look.

"I wonder if you might have known my mother at some point," Tara began shyly. "Her name was Claire Andrews. I don't think she lived here exactly; she might have just come for a summer."

Stella's eyebrows inched up. She pursed her lips and resumed knitting. Tara wondered what had offended her.

Kate whispered in her ear, "Stella's a little hard on the summer people, especially the ones who aren't respectful of our traditions and sacred cows."

"It might have been a long time ago," Tara continued. "My—my mother was only fifty when she died, but she knew Annie's grandmother. I found some letters she wrote to her. I came to thank her for being kind to my mother, but I didn't know she had passed away."

Stella cleared her throat. "The name doesn't ring any bells. Do you have a picture?"

Of course. Anyone pretending to be looking for information about someone would show a picture around. Every daughter had a photo of her mother, didn't she? Tara felt her chin tremble. An unexpected lump rose in her throat. She had only a picture in her mind and the awareness that she was no longer acting. She really did want to know about her mother.

"You can bring a picture next week, Tara," Annie said quietly.

A chorus of voices assured the eagerness of the women to uncover the history of Claire Andrews.

"You said you could stay a while," Annie added. "It will give us time."

Tara swallowed hard. She'd been in Stony Point exactly one week. It had been a surprising ride so far with people who seemed to care about her. What would the passing time bring? Days of pretending, snooping, scheming? If only she could get Jem to forget about the canvases. If she could find work, make some money, maybe he would be satisfied, and they could go away. It was hard to stay focused on Jem's plan when these people around her were being so kind. She hadn't expected to like them so much.

— 8 —

*I*an rounded the corner past Dress to Impress and realized he wasn't—dressed to impress, that is. But it was
Saturday, and even a mayor should be allowed a day to relax
in his most comfortable clothes, hence his ten-year-old
Dockers and faded blue polo shirt. He dropped a hand into
a cozy pocket.

Should a man who'd never played polo in his entire life
wear a polo shirt? He grinned at his trivial turn of mind.
He'd never even known a polo player. He had, however,
played a round of golf at 5 a.m., and managed to beat Ira
Heath and Mike Malone. They were notoriously poor golf-
ers, a fact he chose to ignore today—Arianna's birthday.

He had determined not to dwell on the death of his beloved wife this year. *Stay busy, stay around the good people
of Stony Point*, he had warned himself. But how many years
did it take before you got over missing someone who had all
but made the sun rise for you each morning?

He allowed himself to recall the way she used to adjust
his tie, finishing off the task with a kiss on his chin. The
brain aneurysm had taken her swiftly and cruelly, but she'd
left her touch on Stony Point with her love of theater and
art. Ah, they'd had such plans—plans they made as they
walked along the rocky shore, watching the mist rise in
slow-moving splendor over Butler's Lighthouse.

Enough, he told himself. Be grateful for what is past, but prove its power in a significant present. And life in Stony Point was more than significant. He waved to Scooter who was rushing toward the Gas N Go and tucking his uniform shirt inside his jeans as he ran. His thatch of pale hair flew in the wind. The kid frequently turned up late for work, but his cheerful grin and enthusiasm made for good job security.

"Hey, Mr. Mayor!" he shouted.

That was a teenager's way of saying hello. He liked it. "Hey, yourself!"

He ducked into The Cup & Saucer, eager for the diner's bright ambience and comforting smells. He'd have the works, which meant egg-and-potato scramble with ham. During the week he watched his cholesterol, but it was Saturday.

He greeted the locals and noted several tourists as well. The number seemed to grow each year. And why not? Stony Point was a prosperous little town set in some of the best vacation country in the world. More than that, its citizens were resilient, generous, and proud. And he was honored to be their mayor.

Peggy spotted him and came tripping toward him, coffeepot in hand. Her nails were pink but bore no further embellishment today. Matching pink streaks in her short dark hair revealed that Mitzy, her beautician sister, had been at it again. In her zest for life, Peggy leaned toward whatever was new and off-the-wall, but she charmed everyone and could fill an order in no time flat.

"Morning, Mr. Mayor. You're looking fine!" she chirped. She filled his cup. "The Saturday special?" she queried. "Better get it now. We may run out." Barely taking a breath she rambled on, "Where is everyone coming from? Is the whole world vacationing in Stony Point? Even Wally's—" She broke off, her eyes going suddenly wide.

Ian glanced up. Peggy rarely interrupted her own string of speech.

"I mean ..." She put a pink-tipped finger to her temple. "I mean Wally's had to drop me off early to refill every-thing—the sugars and creamers, the napkin holders, salt and pepper. Everything!" She spun off to get his Saturday special.

Ian grabbed for his coffee, feeling as though a tornado had just ripped through the building. But he felt himself smiling. Peggy could charm the rings off a raccoon. In the booth across from him, Commander Neil Bruce, decorated war veteran and Stony Point's official VFW representative, raised one bushy eyebrow knowingly and gave a half salute. Martha, his diminutive wife, mouthed a "Good morning, Mayor" and daubed her lips with her napkin.

Peggy returned, dropped the Saturday special on his place mat, and slid in beside him. "Speaking of summer people, I suppose you've heard about Annie's surprise tourist," she said in a hushed aside.

When she seemed ready to fly off again, Ian stayed her hand. "Surprise tourist?"

"A girl whose mother recently died. She's kind of lost, and she just turned up at Grey Gables. She practically fainted on Annie's doorstep. Annie brought her to A Stitch in Time for the Hook and Needle Club meeting on Tuesday. She's really sweet looking, but skinny as a knitting needle. Disgusting is what it is. Bet she never gains an ounce!" She recaptured her hand and gave him a little wave. "Gotta run, but hey, there's Annie. You can ask her all about it."

Annie breezed in, wearing something pink and stunning. She gave the crowded diner a roaming glance with those incredible green eyes and caught his glance. He suppressed the urge to smooth his hair as she came toward him.

She'd had that effect on him the minute he'd met her, when she'd first come to Stony Point to make arrangements for her grandmother's estate. He couldn't be happier that she'd decided to stay. He was glad they were friends, but was it disloyal to Arianna—especially on her birthday—to feel his heart beat a bit faster at the sight of Annie Dawson?

Annie too had lost someone special to her. She'd talked often enough about Wayne and her life in Texas. She was alone like him, but at least she had a daughter and grand-children, though looking at her, one would never suspect she was old enough to be a grandmother.

And Ian succumbed. Standing, he pressed a hand across the crown of his head. Not the time for a stubborn cowlick. "Annie, would you join me?"

"Ian, hi!" A pleasant flowery fragrance lingered as she breezed past him into the booth. "I had some errands to run in town this morning, and all of a sudden, a hankering for a cheese danish came over me. I see you're having the potato scramble. Looks good."

"A Saturday indulgence," he said ruefully. "And how are things at Grey Gables?"

"Good. Really good," she said. "I'm thinking about get-ting Wally to do something with the pantry shelves. The kitchen cabinets he refinished are beautiful, and I'd like to get everything up to the same standard."

Lisa, a waitress with a pert blonde ponytail, took Annie's order in the absence of Peggy who was serving a large party of tourists. Annie ordered tea and the danish without consulting the menu. "Milk please, no lemon," she told Lisa with a smile.

"It is really great to have you back, Annie." Ian had worried she might have enjoyed her family so much during the winter that she'd change her mind about coming back to Grey Gables. He'd been relieved when he learned that she'd decided to turn her Texas home into a sort of retreat for returning missionaries. It was like her to do something like that. But sometimes he worried that her enthusiasm to embrace the world made her vulnerable.

"It's good to be back," she said. "I'm looking forward to bringing LeeAnn and the kids back to Stony Point. They love it here." She smiled and glanced away briefly, as though embarrassed by something.

"Well, apparently the word's getting out about our fair city. I've never seen so many tourists." He paused as Lisa set a pot of tea and the pastry in front of Annie. Ian cleared his throat. "Speaking of tourists, I heard you have a guest at Grey Gables. Are you running a bed and breakfast now?" he asked with a grin.

She raised a delicate eyebrow. "Word gets around."

"That's our community. We're nothing if not close-knit," he said drily. "I thought you'd like that description, being a member of the Hook and Needle Club."

"Droll. Very droll. I'm not a knitter, but I guess 'close-crochet' doesn't have the same ring." She grinned and stirred her tea thoughtfully. "I do have a guest," she began slowly. She broke off a small piece of danish and considered it before putting it into her mouth. "Her name's Tara Frasier. She's a young woman who's had a pretty rough time and recently lost her mother. When she was going through some things in her mother's Portland apartment she found some letters. They were from Gram. Tara came to Stony Point to thank her for befriending her mother." Annie paused and studied the remaining pastry on her plate.

"Well, did you know her mother at all?"

"No. The letters were recent, but I gather that Tara's mother visited Stony Point as a young woman. She was just fifty when she passed away. Tara's pretty curious about her mother's life. I think there's a bit of guilt there too, for whatever reason. When someone dies, you always think of the things you didn't do—and the things you did but wished you hadn't." She paused, frowning. "Did you know a Claire Andrews, Ian?"

Ian turned the name over in his mind but came up empty. "Claire Andrews," he repeated thoughtfully. "No. Doesn't ring any bells." He searched her face, as though the information might be written there. "How long does your guest plan to stick around?"

"Not sure," Annie said. "She lost her job. She worked for some sign company in Portland that was downsizing. She said something about staying through the summer."

"At Grey Gables?" Ian asked, surprised.

"Well, she's quick to say she won't impose. She's looking for a place in town, but she doesn't have any money, and I have the room."

He wanted to say she was asking for trouble taking in a stranger, and that he didn't want her getting hurt. But he knew Annie would balk at that. She'd put herself out on a limb before and nearly fell off. The truth was he'd cut off his own arm before he'd let her get hurt, but he couldn't tell her that either. "So you think she wants to stick around just to dredge up memories of her mom?" It sounded harsh, he realized. He gave an apologetic shrug. "Doesn't she have a family or ties somewhere to get back to?"

"She has no family, and as I mentioned, no job. But she's eager to get work, even part time, here in Stony Point for the summer. She wants to pay her way, Ian. Don't be so suspicious!" A twinkle in her eye gentled the criticism.

"Just looking out for our fair city, Annie ... and for you." He touched her arm lightly, and then drew his hand back. She said nothing to this, but a little pink spot appeared in her cheek. Ian could feel the heat rising in his own. Clearly, she was becoming more important than was comfortable— perhaps for either of them.

"I saw an ad in *The Point* for help at Carla's," she said. "Tara likes animals. I was thinking that might be something she could do." Annie gave Ian an inquiring look.

He let his breath out slowly. The flinty woman had earned the nickname by which she'd come to be known. "I'm afraid Carla *Callous* might be a harder taskmaster than your guest bargains for. This Tara sounds ... what's the word? Fragile?"

"It's true that she's not the picture of health, but she may have more stamina than we know. It's worth a try." She took a sip of tea and asked, "What do you know about Carla, Ian?"

"Not much, I'm afraid. She came here four years ago and bought the old Bergner place. Paid cash on the barrelhead. She fixed up a couple of the outbuildings, built a raft of pens and fences, and began taking in stray animals. Came with one or two of her own too, I think. Good thing the area is zoned for farming with all that barking and screeching going on. Still, on a quiet day, I'll bet you can hear the ruckus from your place."

Ian paused, distracted by the sound of Peggy's laughter. From the corner of his eye he saw her chatting with a dark-haired man at the coffee bar. He turned back to Annie. "I do know she can't keep good help. She has a mouth on her that could make a porcupine blush."

"Hmm," Annie said, her brows knitting together. "People who act like they hate the world usually have some deep hurt in their lives."

It was the kind of comment he'd come to expect from her and he recalled his earlier thought about Annie's tendency to embrace the world. "Everyone deserves a second chance," she'd said when Harry Stevens had gotten into trouble over his grandfather's medals. Ian leaned back against the booth. "She's poured a lot of money into those strays of hers. Someone dumps Fido or Calico on her doorstep in the night, and she takes it in. She's gathered quite a menagerie."

"No wonder she needs a bit of help, Ian. You know, the Hook and Needle Club is going to donate proceeds from its next festival for the shelter."

"Don't expect a hearty thank-you from Carla *Callous*," Ian said.

"That's what Stella said." Annie pursed her lips; her eyes

softened. "But you've got to admit, we owe her something for what she's doing for the community. Even if it's not the community she really cares about. And of course, we don't know what's in her mind, do we? We don't know what she cares about."

"We don't," Ian admitted. He paused briefly. "I should add she's not running a full-fledged city shelter. She doesn't have a license or anything yet, though she's working on it. I hear, however, that she's a qualified veterinarian."

"Have you taken Tartan there?"

"Uh—no," Ian said flatly. He'd become more than fond of his patient, sweet-tempered schnauzer with his distinctively bearded snout. "No need to terrify the poor old guy!"

He liked the musical sound of her quick and spontaneous laughter. "Seriously, you shouldn't judge a book by its cover," Annie said. "I think I'll drive Tara out there to meet Carla. Can't hurt."

"Don't be too sure," Ian said with mock seriousness. Then with true seriousness, he said, "Good luck with your mystery tourist, but if you need anything—moral support or anything else, call me."

"I can always depend on you," she said, still with a touch of humor, and he hoped, warmth.

"Promise?"

"Promise," she affirmed.

Ian glanced over to see that Peggy was still engaged in conversation with the guy at the bar. He was a tall, well-built man with hair that hedged his shirt collar. A shiny black lock of hair crept over one eyebrow in the rugged, romantic sort of way he imagined women liked. What little he saw of the face revealed the profile of a man in his late thirties. Ian didn't recognize the man.

As though the stranger had known he was being studied, he abruptly rose, and without turning to reveal his identity, left the diner, but not before placing a generous tip on the counter and exposing a slow-eyed wink in Peggy's direction.

"So, are you going to say goodbye?"

Annie's question jarred Ian. How could he have let one bold stranger distract his attention from her? Not a fair trade at all. "What?" he said distractedly. She had hooked her purse over one delicate shoulder, preparing to leave. "Oh I'm sorry, Annie. I guess I was thinking about something else." He snatched his check and hers, and stood up.

"Oh, you don't need to ..." she began, reaching for her check.

"Want to," he said firmly but with a smile he felt down to his feet. "Let me know how your mystery girl gets on with Carla ..."

"*Calloway*," Annie finished for him, giving him a level look, quickly followed by the laugh he had grown to like so much.

"I'll walk you to your car," he said in a tone meant to prove he had been effectively chastised.

~ 9 ~

"Ouch!" Carla snatched her hand away from the owl's sharp little beak, dropping the fistful of grasshoppers she had brought as breakfast. She hadn't been foolish enough to open the cage door with her bare hands, but Gomer had pierced the flesh on her wrist between the glove and her flannel shirt.

She'd found the barred owl behind one of the sheds, its tibia broken and the toes of one foot badly mangled. In its search for prey the bird had likely been attacked and become prey himself. It was no easy task to affect a rescue. She'd thrown her wool sweater over it to keep it warm, knowing it was likely to be traumatized by the action. Wild creatures often died from shock rather than from their injuries. But the bird had survived. Soon she might be able to release it back into the wild.

Slightly smaller than a great horned owl with no ear tufts, Gomer was brownish in color with broad streaking on its breast. Hence the name barred owl. Its length was about twenty inches and its wingspan about forty inches. She'd named it Gomer for no reason she knew, except that he looked like a Gomer. She pressed the napkin against the sore spot where he'd nipped her and glared into the bird's round face.

"I know you prefer field mice, but talk about biting the hand that feeds you!" She spat the words out, surprised by the level of dismay the creature had evoked. Most of the animals she tended expressed their appreciation for the care she gave them. Of course, they were in large part abandoned domestic animals that people had simply grown tired of.

"You OK?" Vanessa had come in just as Gomer had struck.

"Blamed bird bit me!" she fumed. She pressed a Dunkin' Donuts napkin to her wrist. "Why aren't you out cleaning the cages like I told you to?"

"I finished them," the girl said quietly without looking up. Her drape of dark hair fell over her forehead as she edged toward the door. "I was just going to wash my hands."

"Well, get me a bandage from the back while you're at it. And hurry before I bleed to death!"

Carla turned her back to the teenager who had proved to be her best volunteer yet. She'd had a string of them. Most got tired of the hard work involved in handling shelter animals. They quickly got over being charmed by sweet little puppies and kittens, and left her in a lurch.

Vanessa Stevens worked hard and never made excuses for not coming in. She wasn't lippy either. *Not like most kids these days*, Carla thought. She bit the inside of her lip, sorry for her outburst. She'd better watch herself if she wanted to keep the girl around. But she had to find a way to get more of the animals adopted. What she really needed was someone with computer skills. She needed a website to help find people willing to adopt her ever-growing menagerie. With her reputation around Stony Point, would anyone answer her ad?

"It's a wonder anyone hangs around the way you badger

them." Ian Butler had minced no words when he'd stopped by recently. He'd welcomed her when she'd moved into the area and even facilitated her land-grant deal. He didn't come around much, but she knew he kept an eye on her, like he did anything that had to do with his beloved Stony Point.

"I'm not running a personality contest here, Mr. Mayor," she'd spouted back. "I'm just trying to help the animals your good people leave on my doorstep anytime they get tired of them."

She knew abandoned animals didn't always come from Stony Point's citizens; more likely they were castoffs from summer visitors or area strays. And she knew he was secretly glad the animals were being taken care of. He hadn't flung a bunch of rules about licensing and such in her face. He'd been very patient.

Mayor Butler had pursed his lips and narrowed his eyes at her. "Nobody's holding a club over your head, madam. It's your land."

"You've got that right!" she had huffed and left the handsome mayor standing in the driveway of the country acreage she'd purchased with the last of the Henderson trust fund.

Carla sat down heavily at the makeshift desk with its scattered papers. She kept a log on every animal she took in, and it surprised her now to see how the pile of paper had grown—and how her resources had dwindled. When Vanessa told her she was part of a needlework club and that the group was going to raise funds for the shelter, she'd been even more surprised. What was behind their generosity? People always had ulterior motives.

She'd never intended to come back here, of all places.

As a child she'd been taken to a lot of resort towns and dragged to places she didn't want to go. Mostly she was left on her own or with one of the nannies charged with her care and keeping. Stony Point was just another vacation spot for her wealthy family, but here her life had begun. And ended! After that terrible summer, she dreaded even the sound of its name. So what was she doing here? Was it a kind of self-flagellation? Some twisted sense of impending fate? She shook her head against the memory.

When she left home after her degree from William & Mary, she wasn't sure anyone even noticed. Her father spent most of his time amassing a fortune, and her mother, obsessed with her societies and clubs, found little time for child rearing. What was the point of thinking about it now? They were both gone, her father at the tender age of 55 and her mother ten years later of lung cancer. Carla had been a young woman when they passed away, but she'd felt like an orphan long before their deaths. She fingered her sore wrist.

So what is this, she asked the wary-eyed bird soundlessly, *a private pity party?* She laughed out loud at her thoughts. At the sound, the owl ruffled its feathers and opened its deadly little beak in alarm. What was it the poet Walt Whitman had threatened? To turn and live with animals? Yes, she recalled the lines from her brief sojourn in English literature. It was the same year she'd fallen in love with Ed. He might have joined her quest if he hadn't been sidetracked by a face far prettier than hers and taken off for South America on a wildlife expedition. Likely, Edward Mellinger didn't even remember her anymore.

"This big enough?" Vanessa returned with the bandage. The old chocolate lab with hip dysplasia loped awkwardly behind her. He'd been left at the far end of her property a few weeks before and seldom let her out of his sight. Poor old boy; he'd never be adopted, and he wouldn't be around long. The dog nuzzled Carla with his wet nose.

She took the bandage from Vanessa's tanned fingers. "It'll do," she said, searching for the thank you she knew she ought to say but not finding it. "Did you fill Boomer's water bowl while you were back there?" she quipped.

"Yup." Vanessa nuzzled her face in the dog's velvety fur. She gave his ear an affectionate tug and looked up at Carla. "Gotta go." She glanced at Carla's arm. "You sure you shouldn't see someone about that?"

"It's just a scratch," she said roughly. "Gomer there may have a ton of germs from all those squirrels and mice he's eaten, but he doesn't have rabies." Why did she insist on naming the animals? Simply to inflict more pain when they were gone, to savor it like a hair shirt penance? "Don't forget to close the gate," she added sharply. She turned her back to Vanessa and went into the little kitchen behind her office.

She'd barely finished a ham-and-cheese sandwich when she heard a car pull up. If someone else had come to get rid of a pet she would send them away in no uncertain terms. Dropping her dishes in the sink, she went back into the office.

Two women climbed out of an old burgundy Malibu. The driver looked to be in her forties. She had medium-length blond hair, a quick step and a trim figure—the kind of build that made Carla draw in her expanding waistline.

"You've got to stop eating all those sweets; you'll blow up like a balloon!" Her petite mother's frequent cant when she was a child had only made her crave desserts more. Why did the memory still rankle after so many years? She'd been an oyster in a family of cultured pearls. Well, maybe she liked it that way! She strode to the door and prepared to quickly dispatch whoever was calling.

At least the arms encased in a pale blue sweatshirt held no animal. The woman wore slim jeans. A paisley fabric bag was slung over one shapely shoulder.

"Hi, I hope we haven't come at a bad time. My name is Annie Dawson, and this is my friend, Tara." She extended a hand with a smile and hopeful green eyes. When Carla didn't take the outstretched hand or move from the doorway, she continued somewhat more hesitantly, "I'm a member of the club that's hosting a benefit for your shelter ... the Hook and Needle Club run by Mary Beth Brock."

Carla mumbled something in return, but she had been distracted by the face of the younger woman at her side. Rail skinny with enormous brown eyes, she had dark hair as curly as corkscrews ... a lot like ... *Drat! What is wrong with you, Carla Calloway? Get a grip!*

"Tara is interested in the ad for temporary employment you posted in *The Point*," Mrs. Dawson was saying. "She's good with animals, and she really needs the work right now. I wonder if you might have time to talk with her." Tentatively she stepped away. "I'll just—I'll wait in the car."

Carla recovered. "Sure," she said, aware that her voice sounded more like the croak of a tree frog. Green Eyes had returned to her Malibu, and the young woman was stepping gingerly inside. "Have a seat," she said, pointing to the chair opposite the desk. Her legs felt weak, and her mind seemed to be in some kind of time warp. She pulled an application from her desk drawer and concentrated on its bare whiteness. "Name?"

"It's Tara. Tara Frasier. I …"

"Spell it please."

"F-r-a-s-i-e-r," she responded. "Mrs. Calloway—"

"It's Miss, but you can call me Carla," she said without looking up. "Experience?"

"I don't have any, but I really like animals, and I know I could do the work."

"How do you know?" Carla demanded. She knew she sounded hard—angry even. But it was the memory, that memory that had nagged her for all those years. Why did it come back to slap her in the face just because a young woman happened to look like *her*? Thinking quickly of her own life, Carla wondered what she had hoped to accomplish by coming back here? "If you have no experience you have no idea whether you can do the job or not!"

The girl seemed stunned. Then with a little lift of her chin, she said, "You could at least let me try." The brown eyes darkened. The girl was angry too, or determined. A lot like … Suddenly Carla was sixteen again, and she was with Corky. They were sunning on the beach at Butler Point, the boom box turned up high while they swayed dreamily in their bikinis.

"You can call me Corky if you want to. And you'll be Carlotta," Corky had said. *"Wasn't she some hoity-toity princess or something?"*

"I'm not a hoity-toity princess. Take that back!" Carla had retorted.

Then the memory shifted, and they were walking to the wharf, hoping to be noticed by the lobstermen on the dock who hauled in their catch with brown, muscled arms. Climbing up to the top of the point, they pretended they could fly. Later they would stop by Mrs. Holden's house on the hill for lemonade and homemade cookies. But the summer would end, and knowing it, the pair linked arms fiercely, trying to squeeze the last ounce of adventure before they went back to their boring lives.

"We'll be going home tomorrow. They never go to the same resort twice! What if we never see each other again?" Carla had asked.

Now Carla could almost feel the hot sun on her face, the smooth young arm linked in hers as they walked past Butler's Lighthouse.

"I won't forget," Corky had mumbled.

"Give me one of your curls," Carla had begged.

Corky had allowed her to snip one of her kinky curls with the tiny manicure scissors from her beach bag.

"I'll keep it always!" she had told her friend.

At first, Corky had rolled her eyes, and said, *"You're crazy, Carlotta!"* But then her dark eyes had misted over, and she had kicked hard at a stone in their path.

"I mean it. I'll never forget ..."

Tara's repeated plea jerked Carla back to the present. "Won't you at least let me try?"

Carla dropped her pencil onto the blank page and regained her composure.

"Look, it's more than taking care of animals. What I really need is someone to help with all this paperwork." She swept her arms over the sea of white in front of her. "And I need someone who can operate this blamed computer, to get word out about animals that need homes. Unless you can ..."

"I can," Tara said, interrupting. "I can do that, and I know a lot about advertising. I used to work for a sign company."

Carla faced the young woman across from her, and took in the wild mass of curls and the eyes filled with determination or hope or something else. Her finely etched lips tightened as their gaze held. Whoever she was she had touched some deep place inside Carla, a place that hurt more than her wounded arm.

"Pay is ten dollars an hour, but I can only afford half days."

"That's OK. I'll—"

"I expect you to earn every dime." Carla stood abruptly. "Just because you're friends with that society needlewoman ..." she paused, not knowing how to phrase her thoughts. "I'll accept their charity for the animals' sake, but I don't kowtow to anybody."

She sounded like a shrew even to herself. What must this girl be thinking? Perhaps she would simply bolt out the door and never come back.

"We'll be best friends forever and ever, won't we?" Carla— or Carlotta as Corky called her—slipped the expensive gold ring she'd been given on her fourteenth birthday onto the thin, tanned finger of her friend. Best friends forever! Her heart was big enough to explode. In a few days she would

have to go back—back to the endless parties and socials, the stiff regimen of private tutoring, the emptiness of her heart. And her best friend would go back home too. They'd be separated by so many miles—it might as well be oceans.

"Best friends forever!" she whispered as she twirled the handmade bead ring Corky had given her in exchange around her finger.

Tara had reached the door and was about to go through. Carla felt a wave of panic. "Can you start on Monday?" she called.

Tara turned and her voice came back like a wave breaking over the surf. "I will. And thank you, Miss ... uh ... Carla."

As the door closed, another opened, and Carla stepped again into the past. The sun dropped lower and lower over the bay like a field of wilting roses in a blue china bowl. They had explored the coves and caves around Stony Point and watched the whales breaching in the distant bay. They'd come as close as they dared to the seals, wanting to touch the sleek gray bodies on the sun-drenched rocks. They picked wild daisies and made flower wreaths for their hair. *"He loves me, he loves me not."* Carla could feel the thick curly locks in her fingers as she tucked a wreath into that mass of hair.

"Do you think you'll fall in love, and get married some day? Have kids?" In answer, Corky lay back with her arms flung over her head and stared into the blood-red sky. What was love anyway?

The bellowing and barking from the pens broke through her reverie. Boomer bounded in again, crookedly, pressing his wet nose against her leg. How long she sat there after

Tara Frasier left she couldn't have said, but it was time to pay attention to the four-legged orphans who needed her; time to stop the memories stirred by the girl who looked so much like Corky. So much like the girl who had destined her to a life of unabated guilt.

~ 10 ~

nnie woke to the aroma of coffee brewing. A glance at the clock revealed she'd slept longer than usual; maybe that was because she'd spent several hours in the attic looking through boxes for information about Tara's mother.

She hadn't found any mention of anyone with the name Claire, but she had located a number of small, carefully stored cross-stitch pieces she hadn't known existed. Several pictured cats that might have been inspired by Boots. Annie suddenly realized that Boots had started her day without her—usually the hungry cat pawed her mistress awake. Her mind drifted back to the small cross-stitch pieces; they would be just the ticket for the shelter benefit. They could be framed or inserted in covers of jewelry boxes. As Betsy Originals they'd bring a good price.

She threw on jeans and a light knit top, and headed for the kitchen. Tara had been with her almost a week and a half; she had finally made herself at home as Annie had urged her to do.

She turned around to face Annie when she entered the kitchen. "I hope you don't mind," Tara said. "I started the coffee." She wore jeans and the same blousy top she'd worn the day before. It still looked clean and fresh, so she must have washed it. Her mass of curls was held back with combs, and her complexion shone with delicate color.

She'd come a long way since the night she'd stumbled, ashen and weak, up the hill to Grey Gables. The previous day she'd even insisted on walking the two miles to the shelter "to save you the trouble of driving me."

"I don't mind at all. In fact, I'm glad to take you; I usually have some errands to do in that direction anyway."

Not only had Tara started the coffee, but two places were set at the table, and the butter and jam were in place for toast.

"Will it be cinnamon raisin or wheat?"

"I'll have the raisin. Thank you, Tara, but you don't need to wait on me."

"But you've done so much for me, Annie. I want to help. And just for the record, I'm going to pay you back for all these meals you've been giving me when I get my first check … that is, if Carla doesn't fire me first." She arched her eyebrows and gave a small smile.

Annie slipped into a chair. "And how *did* your first two days go?"

"OK, I think," Tara said, buttering a piece of toast. "I keyed in a lot of records and worked on a website for her; it should be up and running in a day or two. She's hoping to spread the word about the animals in order to find good homes for them. She gave me a bunch of photos to post on the site."

"Wow, you *have* been busy. Did she like the website you designed?"

"Well, I don't think she hated it, but Carla isn't much for compliments."

Annie sighed, understanding. Her encounter with Carla

Calloway had been awkward at best the day she'd introduced Tara. The woman could do with a course on winning friends and influencing people. "She's a strange one," she said. "No one seems to know anything about her really. She hasn't been in town long and has no relatives here ... that we know of. Ian's been out to welcome her; he even helped her with some business details for the shelter. He said she wasn't much for compliments either."

"She hardly talks to me all day, but I can tell she's watching me. It makes me nervous, like she's waiting for me to make a mistake or something. I look up and find her eyes on me. Then she mumbles something and walks away. She yells her head off at Vanessa, though. But I think she likes her."

"Vanessa can hold her own," Annie said with a smile. "And she'll put up with anything to be around animals. It's a shame Kate's so allergic. Bet she makes Vanessa change clothes in the mudroom and shower before dinner after a day at the shelter."

"Carla gives her a huge apron to wear when she's in the pens. That should help some." Tara took a sip of her coffee and added, "The kittens at A Stitch in Time are so cute; are you going to take one?"

"Boots might have a thing or two to say about that," Annie said drily.

As though her name had been taken in vain, the cat left her window seat and leaped up on Annie's lap. "My, what big ears we have!" Annie laughed softly and stroked the silken fur. "Never mind, your kingdom is secure—at least for now."

Annie and Tara finished breakfast in companionable

silence. There was something very likable about Tara, but disturbing too. She couldn't put her finger on it. Perhaps it had something to do with Tara's failure to be straightforward at first about why she'd come. She'd explained it reasonably, and yet … Annie directed her gaze out the bay window where busy sparrows laced in and out of the hydrangeas. What would the mysterious Claire Andrews tell them if she could?

"Tara," she said, pushing her dishes forward and giving Boots a gentle shove off her lap, "I did some searching in the attic yesterday." At the sudden lift of wide brown eyes, she added quickly. "I didn't find anything about your mother yet." She'd feel better about things if she could corroborate Tara's story about her mother. Still, why should she doubt it?

A little silence passed between them. Then Annie corralled her thoughts. "I'm sure between the ladies of the Hook and Needle Club and a bit more exploring, we'll learn something. There's still a ton of stuff to go through up in the attic."

Tara said nothing. She began clearing the dishes and placing them slowly in the drain board. Boots reclaimed her seat in the window and watched through heavy eyes as the sun streamed over her back.

"Tara, would you like to help me with a little project for the shelter benefit? You don't go to work until one—right?"

"Sure," Tara responded, turning.

"I found some cross-stitch pieces of Gram's that are perfect for framing or jewelry boxes. The girls at A Stitch in Time will help too, once the pieces are cleaned and straightened. They're beautiful originals—a lot of them with animals as subjects. We can set up a table upstairs with the supplies. Are you game?"

"I don't know anything about needlework, but I'm willing to learn," Tara said. "I love the picture of the ocean that hangs in the bedroom—with the porch and geraniums and the white sailboat on the water. Your grandmother was such an artist. I bet she made lots of pictures like that ..."

She broke off as though she'd spoken out of turn or something. Tara was a strange mix of mouse and lion. Annie smiled. Perhaps everyone was. "Let the dishes go. I can't wait for you to see the little cross-stitch canvases."

Upstairs, in one of the extra bedrooms, Tara helped Annie set up a table and assemble the things they needed: thick terry towels, a wide shallow bowl for warm water and mild detergent, and the blocking board. The board, which she had ordered from Mary Beth, was covered with heavy-duty fabric that was printed with a grid of squares. Before its advent, Annie had used a towel-covered pine board and a T-square for blocking.

"Actually, a person could pin a canvas to a clean, carpeted floor, but the blocking board is much better," Annie said. "Now all we need are these heavy-duty rustproof T-pins and an iron." She plugged in her Steam Master and moved the dial to the dry setting. Annie went up the steps and into the attic to get the box of small cross-stitch canvases she had found. "Go ahead," she said to Tara when she returned to the bedroom, "take a few out and set them on the table. We'll see which ones are soiled and need a bath."

"Oh, these are beautiful, Annie." Tara traced her finger over a watering can in which a curious kitten peered over the edge. Annie's grandmother had stitched vibrant purple petunias spilling over a clay pot near the kitten. "I'm a novice with my watercolors, but your grandmother was truly an artist."

"Well, these are simple pieces. Her true masterworks are the large canvases. She stitched some of them on ratchet frames. You can buy some wonderful modern frames with two-way rail systems, but Grandpa made the first one for her with his own hands, and it was always her pet frame." Annie had found six finished canvases that had been stored in fancy embroidered pillowcases favored by women in earlier years. Some embroidery spelled out the days of the week, and other cases were bordered with lace.

Tara's gaze rested on the doorway to the attic. "How many do you suppose are stored in there?" she asked, almost reverently.

"I haven't counted," Annie said, laughing. "But Gram was very prolific with her needle. And she stored her canvases in homemade pillowcases, so they wouldn't get damaged. I found some others wrapped in acid-free tissue and kept in cardboard tubes. I'm still in the process of going through things; Gram lived a long time, and she was seldom without her needle."

Tara took the watering can and kitten piece out of the water and rolled it in a thick towel, as Annie had showed her. She was about to pin it to one end of the blocking board when the doorbell rang. She jumped at the sound.

Tara had exhibited such skittishness from the start. She acted a lot like Boots when anyone came to the door, Annie thought, amused. The day Boots had knocked the pot of geraniums off the porch, Tara had practically jumped out of her skin. "That's just Wally," Annie said gently. "I asked him to come and have a look at my pantry; it desperately needs new shelves. Come on down. I want you to meet him."

"Morning!" Wally called before she had opened the screen door. He was dressed in his usual blue shirt and faded jeans, his handmade toolbox clutched in one deeply tanned hand. He smiled shyly and lowered his head.

"Oh!" Annie said in surprise, for he wasn't alone. A tall, muscular man, somewhere in his late thirties, stood beside Wally. Unruly black hair dipped over one of his deep-set eyes, giving him a roguish look. But his smile was as broad as his shoulders.

"This is my brother, Je—J.C.," Wally said, dipping his head toward the man. "He's visiting me and Peggy. He said he wanted to see Grey Gables again. Hope you don't mind."

"Not at all," Annie said. "I'm pleased to meet you." She shook his hand and looked up inquiringly. "You've been here before?"

"A very long time ago, I'm afraid. My—uh—business keeps me on the move, but I spent some good years here in my youth. I remember your grandmother. And I'm very pleased to meet you too."

Annie stepped back to admit them, charmed by the stranger's rather over-gallant manner. At least he didn't have any trouble expressing himself. She turned, aware that Tara had followed her obediently down the stairs. "Wally, I don't think you have met my guest."

A deer-in-the-headlights stare passed over Tara's face. She looked as though she might break and run. She was skittish indeed.

"This is Tara Frasier," she said to Wally, who had placed his toolbox inside the hall and was wiping his boots on the mat. "Tara met your Peggy at A Stitch in Time the other day. Now she can meet you and your brother—J.C. is it?"

"Folks in town might remember me as Jeremiah, but the name's a little hard to get around. J.C.'s simpler. Besides, some folks might not want to remember the wild kid I was in those days. I hope I've improved." He laughed, setting off a spark in his deep-set eyes.

Tara didn't move to take the hand offered to her but nodded stiffly, her face drained of color.

"Pleased to meet you too, young lady," said Jem. Turning away, he clapped his brother amiably on the back. "Yup, old Wally and me had some good times here in Stony Point."

Annie suppressed the urge to correct his grammar, which detracted from his charm.

"When we weren't getting up to mischief we did an errand here and there. We liked doing chores for Mrs. Holden. Fine lady. And this house ..." He made a sweeping gesture and looked around the room in open admiration, his eyes coming to rest on the large over-the-couch canvas of flowers. "This house is still an eye-popper—inside and out."

Annie turned to Tara who hadn't moved from the spot. "Tara, will you see if there's still some coffee in the pot?" She gave her a reassuring pat on the arm and turned to her guests. "Won't you come in and have a cup of coffee?" She indicated the way to the kitchen. "I might have some oatmeal cookies in the cupboard. Tara and I were working on something upstairs, but a morning coffee break would not go amiss, would it, Tara?"

"That would be great," Tara said, hurrying away to busy herself at the counter.

By the time they were seated around the table, Wally and Jem were reminiscing about their days hauling lobsters in the old dory that belonged to Wally's dad. Not surprisingly, Jem did most of the talking. Tara had recovered and had gotten cups down from the cabinet above the stove.

"Wally is a fine craftsman," Annie said. "You can be proud of your brother. What line of work are you in, J.C.?"

"Real estate," he replied, and then he stroked his jaw thoughtfully as though contemplating what to say. "As you know, things have been a little slow, what with banks not wanting to make loans, but it will pick up. Already has, as a matter of fact. I look for the market to rally any day now."

"Ayuh," Wally put in. "J.C. had an import/export business before that. He ..."

"So, I thought it would be a good time for a little R and R," Jem said, ignoring Wally's remark. "And what could be better than the coast of Maine in the good old U.S. of A.?"

Annie noticed the way Tara's fingers trembled on the coffeepot. If a couple of visitors could get her so rattled, how did Tara cope with Carla Calloway, pit bull of the animal shelter? Or was it just men who unnerved her? She had said something about a marriage and being abandoned. Once burned ...

"I've heard that Mrs. Holden's become famous these days," J.C. rambled on. "When I saw that gorgeous picture in the Brown Library I wondered if it was done by the same Mrs. Holden I knew. Sure enough, there was a plaque right next to it telling all about her being from Stony Point and all."

Was it odd that a man like Jem would notice a hand-worked canvas? Maybe he was a collector besides a real estate broker. Annie was sometimes surprised when a stranger spoke glowingly of Gram's talent—surprised but eminently pleased. She felt a lump in her throat and missed Gram anew.

"I suppose there are galleries where you can buy one," he continued. "Sure would be honored to have a Betsy Original hanging in my home someday." Jem's eyes wandered about the room as though he might see one hanging on the kitchen wall. The term "Betsy Original" seemed strange on this young man's lips; it almost seemed that he intruded on some private territory. Perhaps Gram's work was more widely known than she had thought.

"And where is home?" Annie asked, mildly unsettled.

"Portland right now," he said matter-of-factly.

"That's not so far. Do you get over to see Wally and Peggy often?"

Wally, lips pursed, was about to say something, but Jem quickly took over. "I keep pretty busy—lots of travel—but it's something I'm planning to change. I'd forgotten what a first-rate town you've got ..." he paused, "and what charming citizens live here," he added, giving both Annie and Tara a meaningful smile.

"Well, I hope you enjoy your visit." Annie nodded to Wally who had said little. He wasn't much of a talker on any occasion, but he was unusually quiet next to his gregarious brother. Annie felt somehow protective of him and a little sorry to see him lost in this man's larger shadow. "Wally's a regular around here. I couldn't get on without him," she said. "His work is in great demand these days. Maybe he's shown you the model boats he builds?"

As though he hadn't heard, Jem leaned forward in a decisive gesture. "Well, I should be off and let Wally get his work done." He laid a hand on the table just a hair's breadth from Annie's hand. "Thanks for the coffee and for letting me have a look at the old place. You've really fixed it up great."

"Thanks to Wally," Annie amended, unnerved by his intrusive manner and by the blush she felt rising in her cheeks. She sometimes offered her guests a tour of the house, but in J.C.'s case, she decided against it, for no reason that she could name. She rose, and the men did too. "It's been a pleasure," she said. "I'm sure you and Wally will get some fishing in while you're here. And I bet you'll fall in love with that delightful Emily. You won't want to be such a stranger." She led them to the door.

When she turned around, Tara had already started upstairs. "I'll get back to work on the cross-stitch pieces," she called over her shoulder.

Annie cleared away the coffee and cookies, wondering about Wally's smooth-talking brother. Mostly, she wondered about Tara's reaction to the two men. Jem could certainly be a bit overwhelming, but why did she act as though the two were about to swallow her up? What was it that troubled Tara so?

— 44 —

"The wood's right solid on these pantry shelves," Wally said, running his hand over the even planes of light oak. "It doesn't make good sense to replace them. We could sand the gouges and such, and then repaint them to match your kitchen cabinets. Besides, your granddaddy built these, didn't he?" He turned to Annie who stood with hands on hips studying the pantry's interior, her fine brows drawn together in concentration.

This was one lady he liked. She'd been the one who gave him a boost when he really needed it. She was no push-over and demanded good work, but she was quick to praise his efforts. It made him want to do even better. When he'd broken his arm and couldn't work at carpentry or repair, she'd gotten Todd to hire him on with his crew. Recently, she'd suggested he try his hand at crafting toy boats. He loved making them, and people were buying them. He owed her a lot.

"I trust your eye for wood, Wally. Let's go for it, and I love the idea of keeping the integrity of Grandpa's work."

"Good oak's not cheap," Wally said, "but I can get un-finished boards and finish the shelves myself. It'll save some money." He whipped his tape measure from his belt and began to take the measurements. "The door will have to stay off for a few days while I'm working on the shelves."

He looked up to see Annie's houseguest in the doorway. Annie set a canister down on the table and motioned for Tara to join them. "I guess we can put up with exposed food for a while!" she said laughing. "Can't we, Tara?"

Tara looked very young in her jeans and T-shirt with her hair drawn back in a ponytail. A few dark curls escaped the rubber band and coiled around her face. She held a tray of something in both hands. "I came down to get some fresh water for the cross-stitch canvases," she said, addressing Annie. Then catching his glance she said shyly, "Hello."

He nodded to her. "Ayuh."

Wally knew Tara Frasier had been staying at Grey Gables. He guessed she was all right, but Annie was sometimes just too kind for her own good. From the corner of his eye, he admired Annie's soft wheat-color hair and the way she moved gracefully as she carried plates from the cupboard to the kitchen counter. He felt a strong need to protect her—like when he'd beaten the stuffing out of that guy who had pretended to be some fancy antiques dealer but was nothing but a two-bit crook.

"Anybody home in there?" Ian Butler peered through the back screen door. "I brought the catalogs you wanted from the Cultural Center."

"Ian!" Annie opened the door, quickly pressing her hand over her hair. "I didn't expect you until this afternoon."

"Have a two o'clock meeting at the town center—some urgent business the board can't seem to put off. So I thought I'd better bring these over now as promised." He stepped in and placed a stack of books and magazines on Annie's counter. "Morning, Wally," he greeted him. "Hard at work, I see."

"Ayuh," he acknowledged.

"There's coffee left," Annie said a little breathlessly. "I can bring it out onto the porch. Things are a bit messy in here."

"Had my fill of caffeine for the morning, but I wouldn't mind a glass of something cold." Ian rested an arm on the counter and smiled at Annie.

"No problem. I can mix up some lemonade, Annie said. "Tara, will you get the red tin from that cupboard? Wally, you come on out too, and have some refreshment."

"I want to get this door off first and finish these measurements. I'll come out in a few minutes." Wally smiled to himself. Annie always tried to include him. She never made him feel like the hired helper he was. But he didn't want to intrude on her conversation with Ian. Besides, he had a sneaking hunch the two had a particular liking for each other.

Ian was a good man. Wally liked his down-home attitude; no fancy airs for him. His dress was casual too, though he kept his gray hair neatly trimmed and his pants pressed—except when he took off in one of Todd's boats on a Saturday morning to haul lobsters. *A real man's man,* Wally thought. He'd been alone a long time after Arianna's death. It had hit him hard. He deserved someone as nice as Annie Dawson. Wally was sure of that. He moved the pantry door aside and propped it up against the counter.

"You go on. I'll get the lemonade," Tara said to Annie. "I think I can find the pitcher."

"Even I could find a pitcher," Ian said drily, looking around the gathering chaos of the kitchen. "The whole world will know what's in your pantry, Annie. Nice to see you too, Tara." He nodded in her direction. "How are things going at Carla's?"

"OK," she said quietly.

"The old girl's not browbeating you, is she?"

Tara often looked like she carried the weight of the world on those thin shoulders. *She's one of Annie's strays, no doubt,* Wally thought. *Well, at least she's doing some work for her keep.* At Ian's comment, a hint of a smile touched the girl's usually serious face. "No. In fact, she's been really nice to me, and I appreciate the work."

Ian's eyebrows went up a notch. "Nice? Are we talking about Carla?" He gave Tara a penetrating look. "I believe you've worked a miracle."

"See," Annie said, giving Ian a mock punch on the arm. "Carla's not nearly as callous as you think. Come on." She grabbed the tray of oatmeal cookies left from their earlier coffee break and led the way out to the porch.

Wally continued his work, while at the other end of the kitchen Tara emptied ice cubes into a pitcher and searched out napkins. From the open screen door behind him he could hear Ian's and Annie's voices rising and falling on the morning air. The sounds were warm and friendly, and Wally felt good just being there.

He'd come to love the people of Stony Point. In spite of his faults and all the wild oats he'd sowed as a kid growing up here, they didn't look down on him. When times were hard, they stood by him. When Emily had broken her leg they'd made anonymous payments on the enormous hospital bill. Now they were buying up his handcrafted boats and saying how gifted he was! Wally hummed a little to himself and only half-listened.

His ears perked up, though, when he heard Ian talking about some money missing from the Gas N Go.

"I stopped in for gas on my way here this morning. Scooter Hatch looked like he'd lost his best friend." Ian's tone was somber.

Everybody liked Scooter. Wally knew him as polite, friendly and eager to go the extra mile. In a day when nobody got service at "service" stations, Scooter would even offer to wash your windshield. Wally straightened, made a pretense of jotting some figures down on a piece of paper. He took a step closer to the door.

"The Gas N Go came up short when they checked receipts at the end of the day last Friday," Ian was saying. "A hundred-dollar bill that had been placed under the drawer in the cash register was missing. Scooter's being blamed for it. He thinks he's going to get fired."

"Oh!" Annie protested, her voice rising. "Scooter's no thief. He wouldn't do that. He's a really good kid!"

Wally looked up to see Ian massaging his temple, like he always did when he had a problem to solve. "I'm partial to him too, but it happened on his watch. He was alone at the store. They've got one of those old-fashioned registers that don't automatically lock. Scooter likely got busy. You know how things can be on a Friday afternoon when everyone is heading out of town for the weekend and stopping for gas."

Annie's brows furrowed as she leaned in across the wicker table toward Ian. "So anyone could have gone inside and taken the money while Scooter was outside helping customers. Doesn't Stuart realize that?"

"Scooter says the bill was there when he came in after

school, but by the end of the day it was gone. Stuart is furious," Ian said. "You know how unreasonable he can be about money. You'd think a hundred dollars was a fortune."

"Well, it would be to Scooter if he has to replace it," Annie was saying. "Almost every penny he makes goes to help his family. With his dad out of work and his mother so sick, he's scraping to help keep food on their table."

Wally felt his knees grow weak. He turned away, dropping to the floor to measure the lower shelves. Last Friday—he had been to the Gas N Go that day—along with Jem, who'd met him in town. They were going home to one of Peggy's fried-fish dinners. Wally felt his stomach turn over as he recalled the afternoon. He had an hour after finishing a woodworking job to take his peapod out for a turn on the bay.

He liked being under the great blue sky with the water swirling around him, whispering its secrets, calming him. The gulls' keening was like strange other-worldly music. Sometimes he felt closer to God in his peapod than anywhere else on earth. But he still came to listen to Reverend Wallace on Sundays. Peggy would have his hide if he didn't. But Friday, Jem at the Gas N Go ... Wally's pleasant thoughts of drifting in the sun cooled as he thought about that day.

When he'd gotten to the end of the wharf around five o'clock, Jem was waiting, hands in the pockets of his trousers, the wind ruffling his hair. He needed a haircut, Wally realized, and he was still wearing those beat-up old shoes that looked like rejects from a thrift store.

"Hey, bro. Thought I'd take you up on that invitation

to dinner." He slapped Wally on the back, and the two headed for Wally's truck.

"Sure," Wally said, recognizing the sour smell of liquor on Jem's breath. He couldn't get the hang of calling him J.C. and had stopped trying. For a man who apparently had lots of business contacts to make along the coast, he was showing up a lot in Stony Point. He was dropping in at The Cup & Saucer too. He frowned. Peggy was always going on about J.C. this and J.C. that. "How are things going?" he asked quietly.

"Swimmingly," he answered. "And with the prospect of one of sweet Peggy's fine meals, I'm a happy man."

"Happy" was not a word Wally had ever connected with Jem. He seriously doubted it was true now. When they were kids, Wally had idolized his older brother; he'd been deeply hurt when he drove away, but relieved too. He didn't have to keep up anymore or make excuses for him.

"Say, I don't suppose you'd like to stop in at the Shark's Head before dinner?" Jem said.

"I don't have time for that anymore, and no taste for it either," Wally said. "I told you; I'm a family man now. And you should lay off that stuff too. It'll kill you."

"You lecturing me, little brother?" Jem's smile remained, but his eyes had turned dark.

"I'm talking to you like a brother," Wally said, surprised at the heat he felt creeping up to his neck. "God gave me a second chance at life," he heard himself say, "and I'm not going to mess it up." A lump stuck in his throat. He was glad they'd reached his truck. He swung the door open. "Come on."

"God?" Jem echoed when he'd climbed in the passenger

side. "You're not lecturing; you're preaching!" he said. He didn't seem angry, though, just amused. Wally had always been the go-along-with-whatever guy, Jem's meek, little shadow.

Jem was quiet for a while and then muttered, more to himself than to Wally, "God never had much time for me."

Wally wanted to ask how much time he'd had for God, but he let the comment rest between them. They were almost up to the Gas N Go, and Wally turned in. The gauge had been hovering close to the "E" mark.

The place was a hotbed of activity. There were lines at the pumps, and Scooter was doing his best to help drivers get on their way. It was Friday, and folks were filling up for the weekend. He pulled up to a pump when the path cleared and got out to help himself. Scooter was busier than a one-armed paper hanger.

"Think I'll go in and grab a bag of chips," Jem said. "Missed lunch, and I'm starving."

He'd gone inside the station and returned with a bag of Twizzlers. Wally slapped a twenty in Scooter's hand as the boy whizzed past, and then they left the Gas N Go.

Friday afternoon.

Now, as the conversation on the porch continued, Wally felt a gnawing in his stomach. Was it possible that Jem had … ? He didn't want to finish the question even to himself, and he certainly didn't want to hear the dreaded answer his mind was supplying. In the old days, Jem had thought nothing of swiping a soda here, a candy bar there.

But Jem was a grown-up successful businessman now. Surely he didn't need to swipe money from a cash register.

Wally caught the inside of his cheek between his teeth. Those days of penny-ante thefts—larks on a summer day— were over, weren't they? But what did he really know about this brother who had left home so many years ago?

Wally packed up his tools and walked out onto the porch.

"Ready for some lemonade?" Annie asked, rising. "Ian didn't eat *all* the oatmeal cookies. Here, sit down."

"I—I think I'd better take a rain check. I forgot ... there's something I have to do." Jem had dropped him off earlier, so he'd have to walk to town or see if Peggy had time to swing by. Either way, he needed time to consider what he'd heard.

"Oh." Annie seemed genuinely disappointed. Her eyes narrowed briefly. "Is everything all right? You look a little ..."

"I'm fine," Wally managed. Annie had a way of seeing into a person, and Wally didn't want her to look just now. "I'll be back in the morning to work on the pantry. Is nine o'clock OK?" He reached for his toolbox and made a show of straightening the bill of his ball cap.

"Sure," Annie said. "And thanks for all you're doing. I can't wait to see the new and improved pantry."

"See you, Mr. Mayor," Wally said. He could do with a little time to think. But the direction his thoughts were taking filled him with dread.

— 12 —

Tara quickened her steps as a low growl warned of coming rain—a sudden tempest on a Monday afternoon. She peered up at the fast-moving clouds. If she had accepted Annie's loan of her bike today, as she sometimes had, she could have made a mad dash to Carla's. But she had wanted the time to think, so she'd set off on the two-mile trek to the shelter, and that with no umbrella.

When she left Grey Gables, the sun had been smiling in a benign blue sky. She'd slept well in spite of worrying about Jem's impromptu visit to Grey Gables last week. It was unnerving when he popped up unannounced like that. Things had been going so well. That day she had finished helping Annie prepare cross-stitch canvases for the Hook and Needle Club to frame. They had listened to comforting music and talked while they worked. She had never had many friends—certainly none like Annie.

Tara smiled, remembering how good it felt to be there— helping to restore the beautiful handwork of a real artist. Together they had washed the soiled pieces, pressed and stretched them, and then, when they were dry, carefully wrapped them in acid-free tissue paper. It was a work of love for Annie, she thought, remembering how tenderly Annie's fingers had traced the lovely designs and the precise stitches. They had been worked with love too. What *was* love like that?

Tara couldn't understand it. She'd felt a bit like an outsider watching Annie, but Annie had quickly drawn her in, trusting her with the remarkable cross-stitch canvases.

As she quickened her steps, Tara marveled that she had been accepted into Annie's circle of friends. She was even learning how to knit, thanks to Mary Beth, who had decided that knitting suited Tara's personality better than crocheting. *But they know nothing about my "personality,"* she thought as the first scant drops of rain fell on her face. They didn't know that the person who had shown up on Annie's doorstep was actually an interloper, and that she was part of a scheme that would violate all the trust that Annie had placed in her.

When Jem had appeared at Grey Gables with Wally, Tara thought she would faint right there on the spot. What did he think he was doing just walking in like that? He'd told her he would stay out of sight, that he'd pretend they didn't know each other. Then he just popped in without warning—drank coffee in the kitchen and sweet-talked Annie like he'd known her all his life. Jem could be so exasperating. Had she covered up her initial shock upon seeing him? Did Annie suspect anything?

Suddenly, as she neared the stretch of woodland on the outskirts of Carla's place, she heard footsteps behind her. She whirled around and felt Jem grab her wrist. He pulled her off the path and into a stand of trees.

"Caught you!" he said, laughing, and tried to pull her into his arms. His skin was hot from running and damp with sweat and rain. She detected the sweet-sour smell of beer on his breath—in the middle of the day. *Oh, Jem.*

She pushed away from him. "What are you doing!" she demanded, anger rising in her. "You can't just keep popping up and scaring me out of my wits like this."

"Come on, baby. I missed you," he said, backing her against the rough bark of a tree. His voice was husky but insistent, dark eyes lit with humor. "Haven't you missed me?"

"No. How can I miss you when you keep jumping out at me?" Her heart thumped like a wild thing in her chest, but she leveled her gaze at him. "Showing up at Grey Gables like that wasn't smart either."

His eyes narrowed, and she knew she'd touched a sore point. Jem didn't like being told what was smart and what wasn't. Sometimes he just didn't think! He took a step back but kept his hands pressed against the tree trunk on either side of her, effectively pinning her there. "I told you I'd be watching." He paused, and considered her as though trying to be patient with a stubborn child. "Besides, what could be more natural than getting to know my brother's friends? It's a bonus to learn Wally's such a regular around there."

"And how did you get here?" She looked anxiously around for the sleek rental car he'd been showing up in. What had he done with the old conversion van?

"Takes money to rent a car—and my cards are maxed." He glared at her to make his meaning clear. It was her fault; she was moving too slow.

"But we can't be seen together. You said—"

"I said I'd be nearby, and I'd be watching." A muscle in his jaw twitched. "Your rich friend doesn't suspect a thing."

She recalled the day he'd nearly been caught snooping around Grey Gables. Boots had been blamed for the downed flowerpot. It was a really stupid move. Sometimes, Jem just didn't use his head.

"What I want to know is what you've discovered in that attic, so I can figure out how to make our plan work," he said evenly. "You've had plenty of time to find the stuff we're looking for." He drew his lips together like a petulant child and glared at her, waiting for her answer.

"Jem, I can't just go rummaging around in there, even if I knew exactly what to look for. It's just not that simple." She squirmed out of his grasp. "I have to go to work. I'm going to be late."

"What are you doing that's so important?" He made no move to touch her but leaned back against a tree, facing her. He folded his arms across his chest and looked at her through heavy-lidded eyes.

"I'm making some money the way people are supposed to make it. I'm working." Jem had held a number of jobs, none of which lasted long. It was always someone else's fault when he was let go. Why couldn't he just settle down instead of thinking up new schemes to get quick money? She thought about Wally, how carefully he set about his work, how much Annie appreciated him. How could two boys who'd grown up together be so different? She drew in a quick breath. "Annie got me this job, and I'm not going to mess it up."

"So, it's 'Annie' is it? You've gotten pretty cozy with the rich lady, haven't you?" His lip curled in scorn but quickly turned into a sly smile. "But that's good. Cozy is good. You just keep it up. Stay on her good side." He leaned toward her, dark hair falling over one eye. "Once we get our hands on those canvases, we'll have some real money, and we can go away together—you and me."

She kept her eyes down. She didn't want to be moved by that little-boy posture that always got to her. She was tired of the pretense, of wishing and hoping. She let out a long breath. "Jem, we don't need to do this. I'll have some money on Friday. You can have it—all of it. I just don't want to do this anymore. I don't want ..." Her throat ached, and she felt the tears gathering. He would try to take her in his arms, comforting her like he always did, and she would crumble like a house of cards. If only she were strong like Annie.

Annie had survived many losses in her life—her parents, her beloved husband, her grandparents. She'd struck out on her own in a new town with people she didn't know. And she had remained strong through it all. Tara thought about the cross-stitched lighthouse she had washed and pressed. The design showed dark waves cresting a rocky shoal, and from the lighthouse, yellow light radiated in a steel gray sky.

"A person can stay strong through trouble by doing what's right, Tara ... and by opening your heart to others." Annie had smiled gently with those words and looked off into some distance that Tara couldn't see.

But knowing what was right wasn't always that easy. And opening your heart could be dangerous. Tara swallowed, realizing that Jem had gone very quiet. No cajoling; no attempt to embrace her.

It was silent in the little grove except for the rain, still gentle, whispering through the leafy boughs above them. Jem remained with his back against the tree, arms folded. They were so close she could see the little black hairs in the hollow of his throat quivering with the rising and falling of his breath. Her own breath seemed to have stopped.

She looked up to see him studying her, the expression in his deep-set eyes hard to read. His pupils were dark, and his mouth rigid. From far away a gull cried. Jem suddenly dropped his arms, turned away, and disappeared into the trees.

She listened for his retreating footfalls, but she heard only silence. The rain, too, had stopped, as though it had been startled back into the heavens from which it came.

A terrible emptiness gaped inside her. She was alone, more deeply alone than she had ever felt. She stepped away from the tree and moved out of the woods, putting one foot in front of the other. But the ground beneath her seemed without substance. She began to run … faster and faster. This was how an empty person moved. She cleared the distance to the animal shelter in what seemed seconds. Perhaps she was, in fact, without substance herself—a ghost.

The barking of the dogs grew louder and more insistent as she approached the large farmhouse. They always made a racket, but the sounds were different—sharp, urgent. She could see them pacing and jumping in their pens. The closer she came, the more boisterous their complaints. It was Vanessa's day off, but in her absence Carla would have fed and watered her charges long ago.

Drawing alongside the pens, she realized that the metal water pans on the concrete slabs were empty. Food dishes had been scattered, some of them turned upside down. She stood still, listening and scanning the area, but there was no sign of Carla. Chilled by the brief rain and Jem's dismissal, Tara shivered.

She ran past the pens and headed for the rambling farmhouse where porch lights still burned at nearly one o'clock in the afternoon. Where was Carla?

She opened the unlocked screen door and stepped inside. The front part of the house had been made into a kind of office that was more like an old country kitchen. The computer loomed on a great round table, surrounded by several wire baskets for records. There were books on animal care, assorted pens and pencils—Carla was not known for tidiness. Four wooden chairs surrounded the cluttered table that served as a computer desk. Carla's desk loomed in one corner, a rambling thing with big drawers, but Carla liked to have everything at her fingertips. She knew "exactly where everything was."

"Hello?" Tara called idly. "I'm here." She draped her wet jacket over a chair and straightened the file folders. She cleared the area around the computer and prepared to continue her work from last week. She was anxious to get busy; she didn't want to dwell on the meeting with Jem and the way he'd simply left her, the hurt and anger plain on his handsome face.

An eerie silence pervaded, mixed with the muffled braying of dogs. Maybe Carla was out in the back preparing the feeding run that Vanessa usually took care of. She herself had never done it; Carla had made it clear that Tara was needed in the office. In the two weeks since she had worked at the shelter, she'd been tied to the computer. Maybe Carla was in her quarters behind the burgeoning office. She wasn't the welcoming type, though she hadn't fulfilled the dire prophecies people had predicted. It was true that she watched her like a hawk, but with eyes more curious than critical. Sometimes a soft half-smile would transform her harsh expression. Then, catching Tara's glance, she would look away.

The minutes passed. Something didn't feel right. A rustling came from the hallway leading to the kitchen where the barred owl resided. Carla kept Gomer in a large cage while its feet and toes mended. Tara peered around the corner. The bird stared at her, angry eyes oddly glazed. It opened its beak as though it would say something, but only a strange guttural sound came out. She shivered again and kept her distance. She'd be glad when Carla released the owl. Who knew what diseases the thing might be carrying? She'd learned diseases could be passed from vertebrate animals to people. They were known as zoonotic diseases, but she'd had no experience with such things.

She settled herself in the chair by the computer and focused on the website. She had to calm herself after the encounter with Jem. Was he angry enough to leave her this time? If only she'd never heard of Stony Point, Maine. If only they hadn't come here, and she'd never met Annie Dawson. And yet …

"Pay attention to that Annie Dawson; she's got an honest heart." Carla had said those words out of the blue recently—Carla, who didn't even seem to like Annie, who didn't seem to like anyone. It was strange.

Suddenly Boomer came scuttling in, his usually perky tail draping the floor. He dragged himself toward her on his crippled hip, whining all the way. He nudged her with his snout.

"Hello, boy," she said gently. She frowned at his continual whining and the odd way he tossed his head. Perhaps he was in greater pain with his hip condition than they'd thought. She'd loved the dog from the minute she'd met him. "What's the matter, boy?" He sidestepped awkwardly and returned to nudge her again. Was he trying to tell her something? She got up and followed.

Boomer led her to a partly closed door off the east end of the long hallway. He pressed his furry weight against the door, flinging it wide.

Tara sucked in her breath. There was Carla on her back on a rumpled bed. She lay eerily still, her complexion drained of color. She was fully dressed in jeans, and the floppy plaid shirt she often wore had become twisted on her stout, muscled body. Graying blond hair had pulled away from its tether, and a few strands strayed across her lined forehead. In that prone position she looked old beyond her fifties.

"Carla!" she whispered, drawing close to the bed but stopping short of touching her. Her arms were flung out and hung limply over the narrow bed. Her eyes fluttered briefly, and faint groans escaped her lips.

A cluttered table by the bed held spent tissues and glasses, a bottle of cough medicine and a sticky spoon. She'd had a slight cough when Tara had seen her on Friday. Over the weekend she must have gotten worse and was treating herself for some kind of respiratory problem.

"Carla, can you hear me?" Then Tara spotted the wrist that had been bandaged after the scrape with Gomer. Ugly and red, it had swollen to twice its size. She raced down the hall for the telephone and dialed 911. Quickly, she gave the location and described Carla's condition. She told them about the owl and the bite and Carla's swollen wrist.

Urging them to hurry, she went back to the bedside, carrying the cordless phone with her and answering the emergency dispatcher's continued questions. Boomer sat with his big head on Carla's blue-jeaned thigh. Carla seemed only barely conscious, occasionally muttering something unintelligible in a breathy tone. "Sorry" was the only word Tara could make out.

"Help is coming. It's going to be OK," Tara whispered. Her voice sounded odd, far away. What more could go wrong on this terrible Monday! She wished she knew how to pray. Dampening a cloth she touched it to her boss's hot forehead, thinking how much the crusty Carla would bristle at such attention if she had been her usual self. "All prickles and stings." That's how Alice described her. And Stella Brickson had harrumphed and offered, "You'd need a tank to get through that woman's defenses!" But Tara recognized something in her new employer—a deep place where pain kept her prisoner as surely as the bars in Gomer's cage.

At the whine of an approaching ambulance, Boomer sat up, and the dogs in their pens barked and brayed with renewed vigor. Relief flooded Tara as she ran to beckon them. She pulled Boomer back and wrapped her arms around him as the EMTs quickly attended to their patient.

Tara answered their questions as best she could. They strapped Carla to a gurney and took her away. Someone would come to pick up the owl, they told her. It didn't look quite right, and the bite might have something to do with

Carla's illness. Tara knew that wild birds carried organisms that could be potentially infectious to humans. A person could experience respiratory illness from flu-like symptoms to pneumonia. Some cases could have serious complications.

Trembling, she dialed Annie's number at Grey Gables. "I'm going to stay here," she told Annie after briefly describing Carla's condition. "Vanessa's off today, and someone needs to see to the animals. I don't know when they were fed; they're making a terrible fuss."

"Thank God you went to the shelter today," Annie told her. "I'll call Vanessa and ask her to come out and help too."

Tara felt herself relax a little as she heard Annie's quiet, confident voice. *An honest heart. Strange,* she thought, watching the ambulance dissolve into a tiny distant speck. Carla had treated her rather shabbily when they'd met, but in spite of it, Annie was quick to help when she was in trouble.

Tara grabbed the sheets and blankets that had fallen from the bed. They would need laundering. She began tidying up the messy room, scooping up newspapers and soiled dishes, feeling the invasion of Carla's privacy as her own. *Too late for embarrassment,* she told herself dismally. A copy of *The New York Times* on the crumpled bed lay opened to the daily crossword puzzle, which was nearly finished. Tara had tried one once, but found it too difficult. So Carla Calloway was something of a brain, she thought, opening a window to let in the fresh air. She straightened a curtain panel that had come loose from its mooring.

As she bent to tuck Carla's slippers under the bed, a bit of yellowed newspaper on the floor caught her eye. She was about to set it on the dresser when something fell out onto the floor. It was a small beaded ring that might have been handmade—tiny red, yellow, and blue beads strung onto plastic wire. Curiously, she opened the folded paper; it was brittle to the touch. Tucked inside was a swirl of black hair—one perfectly coiled tress.

The clipping was no bigger than a postcard, and one short article had been circled in pencil: *An unidentified teen arrested earlier this week after stealing H.T. Simmons's automobile and crashing it into a tree on Ocean Drive remains in custody. The girl's mother, sole parent and resident of Chelsea, Mass., near Boston, was killed in a traffic accident en route to Stony Point. The girl is being held by juvenile authorities pending contact with other family members. Authorities are not releasing further information at this time.*

Other brief articles accompanied the circled story: *Lobster catch diminished by successive days of impenetrable fog. Meeting of the Stony Point Historical Society postponed during repairs.* Tara searched the clipping, but the date was obscured. Feeling like a voyeur, she refolded the newspaper and tucked in the beaded ring and the swatch of hair. She nudged it gently under the bed near Carla's slippers.

So Carla was a bit of a romantic too. It was strange to think of the crusty old woman that way. Who did the hair belong to? And who was the teenager who had been arrested? Was it Carla herself who had stolen the car? How tragic to lose one's mother like that. She pulled the newspaper out again and reread the paragraph, registering the details in her mind. Who was H.T. Simmons? Did he get his car back? What happened to the unidentified teenager whose mother was killed?

THE STOLEN CANVAS 143

But it was all none of her business; she shouldn't even be reading it. Nerves quivering, Tara picked up the soiled laundry and closed the door to the bedroom. Whatever Carla Calloway's secrets were, they were hers alone.

Tara sighed, feeling desperately weary and at odds with herself. She didn't think she could settle down enough to work on the website or to do the filing that waited in one of the wire baskets. Vanessa would arrive soon; together they'd make sure the animals were fed and watered, but then what?

Boomer traipsed after her, whining softly.

"I know, boy," she consoled. "It's been some day!"

～ 13 ～

Wally thanked Emmet Plait, Todd's right-hand man, who signed out the dory he was to borrow for the day. The loaner was a muscular craft with deep gunwales and a high prow. He'd take her real easy on the trip back with the supplies he needed, but he looked forward to heading out onto the bay and feeling the wind through his hair. He might even have time to look for cliff sparrows or a tri-colored heron with the binoculars he kept in his tackle box. He took a deep breath of sea air and felt his spirits lift.

He needed a couple more three-foot oak boards to complete the job on Annie's pantry. His truck was in the shop. Besides, it was more convenient to pick up what he needed by boat since the mill was located up the coast halfway to Petersgrove. Wally grinned at his rationalization as he prepared to launch the dory. Given the choice, he'd take travel by sea over land any day!

When he was a kid, he had depended on the sea to provide some sanity in his life. When Pop was too drunk to navigate the sound and work his traps, Wally would take the boat out into the middle of the bay alone. Sometimes, idling there under the sky, he imagined his mother calling. He learned to listen for her accents in the keening of the gulls as a soft wind ruffled his hair and swept across his cheek like a caress.

One day, he tried to tell Jem, "Listen! It's like she's here!"

"It's just the stupid gulls—rats with wings!" Jem only laughed and called him a baby. After that, Wally kept it to himself.

He didn't imagine he heard her voice anymore. Still, peace poured over him like a benediction when he glided through the water. He felt satisfied there, whole. But feeling that way had a lot to do with Peggy and God's gift of their sweet Emily.

Peggy would be at The Cup & Saucer, dashing about to fill orders, that smile of hers lighting up the diner like a strobe light. Something nagged at the back of his mind as he thought of her. Hearing how frequently Jem stopped in for coffee bothered him. He was staying in Petersgrove, said he had business there, but he showed up a lot in Stony Point.

Peggy had never given him reason to be jealous, even though she often referred to her customers in that super-friendly way of many waitresses. *More coffee, sweetie? What can I get for you, dearie? Anything for dessert, honey?* Peggy loved everyone and rushed to the defense of the world, but she was his alone. Still, he knew how charming Jem could be. How he could wow the girls and get them to do anything he wanted. Just yesterday Peggy had told him, "Your brother left a five-dollar tip for a cup of coffee and a doughnut."

Well, if he can afford five-dollar tips, he didn't need to swipe a hundred-dollar bill from the Gas N Go, Wally thought. So maybe he could put his mind to rest on that score. Maybe. Recalling the conversation between Ian and Annie brought a quick shudder of dread. He and Jem had been only two of the many customers visiting the station that Friday. Any of them could have done it. Why zero in on Jem? Why did he still see his brother as the unruly kid with a chip on his shoulder—a kid who lifted things from unsuspecting tourists and regulars who weren't watching?

Even after all these years, Wally could picture the watch Jem had stolen with uncanny accuracy. It was a two-toned Rolex—yellow gold and stainless steel—with a silver dial and shiny markers. Gold hour and minute hands glistened in its face with a date window at three o'clock. The gold band had flexed easily in Jem's fingers. "Where'd you get that?"

Jem had quickly stuffed the watch into his pocket and shrugged. "Got it off some guy I took on an all-day fishing trip. He needed a guide—somebody who knows the waters like the back of his hand."

A Rolex, even 20 years ago, cost a pretty penny, Wally knew. A lot more than the usual few bucks the summer people would give for an afternoon jaunt, especially to a tadpole like Jem, whether he knew the area or not. He didn't remember what had happened to the watch after that long-ago day. It surprised him now that the memory had come back so vividly.

The trip to the mill wouldn't take long, and it wasn't even one o'clock yet. He had asked Peggy to have the ham-and-cheese sandwich ready for him when he stopped by the diner before picking up the boat. He half-expected Jem to be there and was relieved when he wasn't.

He climbed into the dory, dropping a folded canvas aft. After he picked up his supplies, he'd wrap the boards in it to protect them from water that might spray into the boat. The sudden storm that had come up an hour or so ago had vanished as quickly as it had come, and a weak sun bravely chased the clouds across the sky.

He took his time launching the dory, his binoculars slung around his neck. A month ago he'd seen a flock of lingering Bohemian waxwings. Not much chance they'd still be around now, but he might spot a snow goose or a coot. He cruised slowly near the shoreline, feeling the worries begin to ebb as the water rocked beneath him. He liked to take Emily around the bay in his peapod. Sometimes they'd fish or look for birds along the bank; those were the best times, and once again he sensed the goodness of his life in Stony Point. Binoculars poised, he scanned the wooded bluff, alert for a blur of wings or a craning neck.

But what came suddenly into his sights had two legs. A man walked slowly along the bluff, hands shoved deeply into his pockets, eyes downcast. The man's gait was familiar. In a flash Wally recognized his brother. What was he doing so far from Petersgrove and a good two miles from Stony Point's town center? Carla Calloway's spread, with her menagerie of abandoned pets, lay just beyond the wooded rise.

Thoughtfully, Wally dropped the binoculars and stared at Jem. And then he saw someone else. A girl ran in the opposite direction along a footpath toward the animal shelter. He raised the lenses once again and notched up the power. The girl was thin, not very tall, and had a wild bush of dark hair. She was running very fast. Even from three hundred yards off shore he recognized Tara, Annie's houseguest, whom he and Jem had met last week at Grey Gables.

That is, he *thought* Jem and Tara were meeting for the first time. What were the chances that Tara and Jem would just happen to be in this wooded area at the same time? And why was Tara running like the devil himself was after her? Had they met by chance, and had Jem tried to make a pass at her? She was pretty, but she hadn't seemed to appreciate Jem's charming ways the afternoon they'd met; in fact she'd been downright cold toward him. Had he said something, done something to her?

Wally didn't want to pursue that thought. He stashed his binoculars in the tackle box and revved up the motor. When he caught up to Jem, he cut the motor and drifted in toward shore. As he approached, he saw Jem pause along the rocky ledge above him.

"Hey, Jem!" Wally called. He flung the cast rope around a tree stump protruding from the shoal. "Come on down. I'll give you a ride back to town."

Panting with exertion, Jem maneuvered the rocky decline. He grabbed hold of Wally's hand and dropped down unsteadily into the boat.

"Well, little brother, I'm glad you happened along. I hitched a ride in from Petersgrove, but the guy only took me as far as the junction." Jem smiled amiably, but he looked worn and tired. His hair looked like a blown haystack, and his fine silk shirt was wrinkled and smudged. "My rental blew a gasket—probably won't get a replacement until tomorrow."

Wally headed out onto the bay at a mild rate of speed, troubled by what he'd seen. What was important enough to bring Jem to Stony Point today, and why did he look like three miles of bad road? "You OK, Jem?"

"Of course. Just got caught in that little thunderstorm we had." He jabbed at the front of his shirt and smoothed his rumpled hair. "Say, where'd you get this sweet little dory?"

"Todd loaned it to me for the afternoon. I'm on the way to the mill to pick up some lumber for Annie. It'll only take a half hour or so, and we'll head back into town. Were you—uh—going somewhere special?"

"Just to see the old digs. Thought I might kick back with you for a bit, but I don't want to make a bore of myself. If you're busy—" Jem left the sentence unfinished.

"I'm picking up some supplies for the job I'm doing. Glad to have you ride along." Wally eased the dory out into the open but kept the pace slow and steady.

Suspicions nagged at him. Jem wasn't booked into either of the hotels in Petersgrove. Wally had checked, having gone himself to the Schooner's Rest Inn. The clerk had said that Jem had been there but had checked out. He was headed back home when he passed the trailer park and saw Jem getting into an old camper or some kind of van. Jem always came to Stony Point in a fancy sedan. What was he doing in that old rig that looked like it was on its last legs? If he asked Jem about it, he'd be mad as all get out, accuse him of spying on him, which was—after all—the truth.

Wally drew in his breath and let it out slowly. "We did a lot of fishing in these waters," he said awkwardly, focusing on happier times so long ago.

"Reckon we did have some good times," Jem said, "but I don't have much time for fishing anymore." He ran a hand along the gunwale. "Nice of old Todd to loan you his boat." He gave Wally a sly smile. "You're in pretty tight with the good citizens of Stony Point." It sounded like an accusation, and Wally was puzzled. The chip Jem had carried as a boy seemed to have grown into a boulder.

"They're good neighbors," Wally said, "and they've been good to me."

Jem said nothing to this, but just stretched back against the seat and peered into some distance Wally couldn't see.

Actually, they'd been generous to Jem, too, when they could have arrested him after he burned down Homer Swenson's barn. He'd gone in there to smoke a cigarette. He'd had to work off some of the damages by hauling hay for Swenson all summer.

"It's good to have friends, Jem," Wally said thoughtfully. He paused. "That was Annie's friend running along the path a few minutes ago, wasn't it?" He hoped for an offhand manner as he steered, his hand steady on the tiller.

Jem looked up, startled.

Wally knew he was surprised that someone had seen them. "She was running like a mad woman." Wally jerked a thumb toward his open tackle box. "Binoculars. I keep them for bird-watching." He waited for a sarcastic comment about bird-watching, which his brother was likely to think wasn't manly.

"I ran across her on the footpath, but she was too busy to say hello. She—uh—said she was late for work. So much for friendly citizens." Jem gave a nervous laugh. "Then again, maybe I'm losing my touch."

Wally negotiated a bend in the coastline, and they rode in silence for a while. It was hard to figure Jem out when they were kids, and he was a long way from understanding him now. "How come you never came back all those years?" Wally was surprised at the sad sound of his own voice. In spite of everything, he'd loved Jem. "Didn't you ever think about me?"

A frown darkened the handsome face. "'Course I did. I told you, I just got busy. You know how life is. Things pile up on a person; time gets away." After a brooding pause, he leaned over and gave Wally a slap on the shoulder. "Plenty of water's been washing over the bridge for you too, man. You're married and got a kid and all." His voice trailed off, and he squinted up at the sky. "Yeah," he said, stroking his jaw thoughtfully, "a lot of time has passed, but we did have some good times back in the day."

Wally saw that the trousers of Jem's pants were frayed at the hem; there was a break in the sole of his left shoe. Real-estate bonanzas and five-dollar tips aside, maybe he wasn't the tycoon he pretended to be. *Mister, can you spare a dime?* This view of his brother startled and saddened him. Jem wasn't the brightest bulb in the pack, but he must have learned how to make a decent living. Still, times were hard; jobs were scarce.

"You know," he began tentatively, "we don't have much, Peggy and me, but if you need anything ..." Wally hesitated, frustrated by his thoughts and not knowing how to express them. Then he heard himself say flatly, "Jem, tell me you didn't lift that hundred-dollar bill from the Gas N Go last week!"

Several seconds of silence passed; then a gull screamed overhead. He waited, expecting an angry retort or a punch on the arm. Instead he heard low laughter. "Do I look like I need a handout, bro?"

"Well," Wally stammered, "you used to have some pretty

sticky fingers, and then when I heard about the missing money, I just ..." Wally floundered, apologetic and angry at the same time. "You were there with me that day. You went inside the station while I was filling up, and ..."

"So, they got a posse out for a puny hundred bucks from a cash register?" Jem's laughter grew, but there was no humor in it. "Man, this really *is* a two-bit town."

Jem's casual attitude fueled Wally's anger. He blurted out, "The kid working there is being blamed; he might lose his job, and his mother is sick and depends on him." That the money had been in a cash register hadn't been mentioned. Jem had supplied that bit of information. Wally felt his throat thicken, not so much out of sympathy for Scooter, but out of fear that Jem could very well have stolen the money.

The mill's loading dock lay dead ahead. Wally cut the engine and headed in, grasping the tiller so hard he felt his knuckles stiffen. He cast the rope over a bleached post and climbed onto the dock, feeling Jem directly behind him, eager to get out of the boat. He turned back to his brother. "The folks in our town are good people," he said. "I don't want to see them hurt."

Jem's eyes narrowed. Scorn twisted his handsome features into someone Wally barely recognized. "I wouldn't think of offending your precious friends," he said, still smiling in that humorless way. He stashed his hands hard into his pockets and backed away. "Thanks for the ride. And thanks for the vote of confidence."

"Jem!" He didn't want him to walk away mad. He wanted to believe his brother hadn't taken the money. Most of all, he wanted to help Jem if he was in trouble. "Come on back with me, Jem. Peggy will have supper ready."

But Jem didn't turn back. He just kept walking, bobbing from side to side in angry strides. He raised one arm in a kind of farewell salute. Wally was suddenly fourteen again, feeling lost and empty as he watched Jem stalk off.

~ 14 ~

*J*em forced himself to walk and not run as he left the loading dock, past the lumberyard, and into the shelter of trees. He wouldn't look back, though he could feel Wally's eyes on him and hear the soft whine of the dory's outboard motor. He straightened his shoulders and held his head high, anxious to reach the stretch of woods where he could disappear from those accusing eyes.

Blast it all! He'd been so careful. When he stepped into the service station and found the cash drawer open, he'd slipped the bill out from under the drawer without touching the others neatly stacked on top. It was a fierce temptation, but he fought against taking more.

"Tell me you didn't steal that hundred-dollar bill from the Gas N Go."

The charge rang in his ears, and he felt the heat rise up his neck like a creeping flame. You'd think he was a serial killer or something. The town was flush with tourists spending their wads. What were a few bucks? No big deal. Besides, he'd only taken what he absolutely needed. As it was, he'd maxed out his credit cards and could no longer afford a hotel.

He had to sleep in his camper, a jerry-rigged van he'd gotten at an auction. No wonder he hadn't looked fresh as a daisy when Wally saw him. It was hard to look well groomed under such conditions, but he was careful to keep the thing out of sight. It didn't exactly decorate the landscape, and it was important to look successful. He couldn't let people see him driving around in that monstrosity, so he'd rented a car until his credit card had hit its limit.

He'd left the camper at the far end of a rundown trailer park and paid a few dollars for use of the facilities, which, he realized, he needed right now. His shoes were dull and worn, and he hadn't noticed the frayed hems of his pants. He'd have to get some new threads and soon. But he needed the hundred for food, especially now that he would probably be unwelcome at Wally's.

When did Wally turn into such a choir boy? *"The kid's being blamed. His mother's sick and depends on him."* And he had looked at him with those critical eyes, half puppy-dog and half she-bear. The boy's name was Skeeter, Stretch, something like that. He'd seen the spiky-haired kid with the goofy grin pumping gas and wiping windshields. Well, the fool kid deserved losing his job for leaving the register standing open for anyone to pilfer from.

Wally probably believed he was guilty, though Jem hadn't confessed to anything. And he wouldn't rat on him anyway. Would he? They'd been buddies once—two orphans trying to hold things together. *Blast!* He needed to keep on good terms with his brother, to keep his connection to Grey Gables and the valuable canvases. But Wally would be watching him now.

He paused at the edge of town. He was tired, really tired. It was all that traipsing after Tara, and then scrambling down the bank when Wally had called. Drat those binoculars! He hadn't slept well, and his stomach was pleading for attention. What he really wanted was a drink. Wally used to be good for a few beers before he'd turned into another small-town groupie. They'd turned him into one of them, praising him for his fine carpentry and his handcrafted toy sailboats that everyone couldn't get enough of.

"We think a lot of him around here."

Annie Dawson had beamed fondly at Wally, and he'd turned pink around the edges. All because the rich lady of Grey Gables threw him a bone or two now and then! She was using Tara too. Getting her to scrub and clean like a washerwoman. She'd been all sweaty and messed up the afternoon he found her cleaning the stupid chairs on the porch like a common maid. His beautiful Tara with her smooth cheeks and soft lips. And Tara was falling for it. She was eating it up. It was all Annie's fault.

"She's been good to me, Jem. Please, can't we just forget about the canvases? I'll have money by Friday. You can have it all. Only, I can't do this, Jem."

She'd pushed him away as they stood under the trees like he was some monster or something. It was a simple thing he asked of her. Just locate a few of those handworked canvases the old lady had stitched—the ones that were bringing those fancy prices at auction. But she was backing away from him, pleading for him to give up their plans. He was doing this for her too—to give them a fresh start together.

Somehow the people of Stony Point had turned her against him, especially that Annie Dawson with her high and mighty ways. Jem dug his fists deeper into his pockets. *Tara, Tara!* After all he had given her. He'd befriended her when she was all alone and bought her pretty things. He was nice to her. And now she was backing out of their deal.

He kicked at a stone in his path and felt its sharp contours against his toe. He felt suddenly like crying. He wanted to bawl like a hurt child. He thought of Tara's soft arms around his neck, her wild curls crushed against his chest, and he felt the pain all the way down to his sore toe. They were good together, he and Tara; they had good times. She would always be his, wouldn't she? He thought of her lips, gentle against his own, of the way she cared for him when he was sick or tired. And yes, when he was drunk.

Wally was right about one thing. He had to go easy on the booze. It made him a little crazy. Once he'd shoved Tara so hard that she'd fallen against a table and cut a gash in her arm. He could still hear her cry of pain and see the hurt in her soft brown eyes. She hated it when he drank, but a man had to do something to forget. He had to find the strength to face the world. She'd always understood before, even when he'd struck her without thinking. He never meant to. She had to know that.

But she was turning against him now. Just like everyone else. Ever since he was a kid, people had shut him out.

"Didn't you ever think about me?" Wally's sad voice as they drifted in the borrowed dory echoed in his ears.

Yeah, he'd thought about Wally and about the weak old man who'd wrecked his fishing boat one stormy afternoon near Butler's Lighthouse. He thought about old Homer Swenson and the stinking hay he had to pitch all summer long in the heat of the sun. Swenson pretended Jem was getting off easy working like a dog in the August heat—all for one falling-down old barn. Oh yes, he thought about them all more often than he cared to admit. But they'd all shut him out.

People said kids are tough, that they get over things, but they didn't know how a small heart could break and how it could be replaced by something hard as stone that weighed down every step you took and never eased up.

"Your ma ain't coming back," Pop had said, slurring the words. He'd been half drunk, and his eyes were red-rimmed. *"You might as well face up to it like a man."*

His mother was dead. Alive one moment, the next propped up in her coffin. He was ten years old, and he didn't know what a man should feel like. Wally used to hear their mother's voice calling to him on the water. Jem had never heard anything but the gulls mocking him as they swooped overhead, screaming for bread.

As for Pop, all he really wanted was a set of arms to help haul his traps. When things went wrong he always took Wally's side—the baby brother. Jem hated lobsters—those scraggly, creepy things with their beady eyes and hairy feelers. He hated the tourists who spent a fortune for them. He wasn't going to spend his life depending on lobsters for his livelihood. He'd show them all! He'd make a name for himself and come back with enough money to buy the whole town.

He didn't have the money yet, but he would. They'd beg him to come back to Stony Point. Maybe they'd even make him their mayor instead of that haughty Ian Butler who acted like he owned the whole town. Had Butler recognized him that day at The Cup & Saucer? He sat there drinking tea with

Annie Dawson and watched everyone in the diner like they were his personal property or something!

He walked on, approaching Petersgrove and the trailer park. He was glad for the growing cover of darkness. He wanted to get inside his camper where he could think. He just had to play it smart. He had to get what he'd come for and be on his way. He thought he'd keep a low profile and maybe hang around Petersgrove for a little while. But then, he had to keep an eye on Tara. He seemed to be losing control of her now, and he wasn't sure what she would do.

Her words needled him. *"Showing up at Grey Gables like that wasn't smart."*

Sure, he hadn't been to college like the high and mighty Ian Butler, but he was smart enough. He gotten this far—stayed alive—because he had brains. He'd show Wally too. His resolve wavered as a thought flashed across his mind. Wally had already made a name for himself; he'd found a pretty wife who loved him, and he had a child who looked up at him like he was some kind of god.

"God gave me a second chance, and I don't want to mess it up!"

He recalled Wally's startling words, and the way his voice sounded all polite and proud at the same time. What did Wally know about religion? They both used to laugh at the good citizens filing out of church on Sunday mornings. Then they'd discuss what might be in the offering plate and how to latch onto it. The only chances you got in life were the ones you took. It was like everything else—you had to take what you wanted or someone else bolder than you would!

He frowned up into the darkening sky where one lone star winked at him in a kind of mocking way. Yet, his eye was drawn to it, and it made him sad somehow. Wally had a job, a family and the respect of friends. What did he have? At nearly forty he was alone—still on the outside—wondering where he could get a clean shirt and a new pair of slacks. Worse yet, he needed a meal.

How could he spend that hundred-dollar bill in the small village of Petersgrove without raising eyebrows? Everyone around there thought he was a rich tourist spending a few weeks of holiday. Still, it shouldn't be difficult. He just had to think!

"Jem, come back with me!" Wally's words echoed in his mind. He imagined him as an awkward little boy holding a tie rope in his hands. Once when they'd been fourteen and eleven they'd found a fishing boat drifting in the bay. Jem knew it belonged to the Butlers, but he'd rubbed out the fleet number and planned to hide it in the brush behind their house. As they approached shore, he saw the old dockhand waiting, a scowl on his face. Jem jumped into the water and swam away before they reached shore. He'd left Wally—holding the tie rope—left him to face the music alone.

Good little Wally, who'd always stood by him. Even though he suspected his brother was a fraud and a thief, Wally was still reaching out to him, inviting him to his home for dinner. Something in Jem folded inward, threatening to crush him.

No! He jerked his head up. Had he said it out loud? He straightened his shoulders and tucked his shirttail inside his pants. No—he didn't need Wally's charity! He didn't need handouts from a two-bit village like Stony Point, and he didn't need Tara. They'd all pushed him out.

Outsider. Outsider. Nothing had changed. He'd handle things on his own … just as he always had. Wally wasn't going to help him; no God was going to come down from heaven to bail him out. He was alone. And the winking star seemed to follow him, laughing—if stars could laugh.

~ 15 ~

Alice hopped out of her Mustang, wearing white capris and an aqua blouse sprinkled with tiny white flowers. As she approached Annie, she shut her cellphone—a constant appendage on her ear—and climbed up onto the porch. "Your message said that Carla Calloway was taken to the hospital. What happened?" She'd been gone all day to a Divine Décor convention in Wiscasset and was catching up.

She flopped down on a chair and laid her sunglasses on the table. Her turquoise and silver bracelets clinked together as she leaned forward and peered at Annie questioningly.

"You look better in person than on the phone," Annie said, gesturing to a chair. "Sit down," she offered expansively. "Oh, you are down. Well, never mind."

"Never mind the humorous banter! Tell me what's been going on. I leave town for a day or two, and everything falls apart!"

Annie had brought two coffees out onto the porch. She pushed one toward Alice. "Well, it seems that when Tara arrived at the shelter yesterday, she found Carla nearly unconscious in her bed. Apparently, she'd been fighting a cough over the weekend that turned into pneumonia—or something like it."

"What do you mean? Something like it?"

"She got it from an owl. I never heard of it before.

Ornithosis or something like that."

Alice frowned; she made no move to touch her coffee. "An owl?"

"Carla rescued it out on the property somewhere. It had a broken tibia and crushed toes. The authorities quarantined it, of course. She kept it in a cage in the hallway, named it Gopher or Gomer or something like that. The doctors said these wild birds can carry diseases that can be transmitted to humans. They call them zoonotic diseases. Good thing Carla kept the owl out of the waiting or examining rooms, so the other animals should be OK."

"I never heard of such a thing!" Alice said.

Annie shrugged. "Well, I guess the bird bit her. Carla said it was nothing, but she was a pretty sick puppy. She had a high fever and was nearly delirious when Tara got there. It's a good thing she came when she did. She called 911, and then she called me."

Alice blinked, absorbing the information and shaking her head. "Is Carla going to be all right?"

"She should be, now that they know what's wrong. It's a disease caused by the bacteria an animal carries and it shows up usually a week or so after exposure. The infected person experiences respiratory symptoms, but serious cases can result in hepatitis or even inflammation of the heart muscle."

"Wow! Taking care of animals can be downright harmful to your health," said Alice.

"I guess so. I bet Carla thinks twice before taking in wild birds again."

"For sure," Alice agreed. "By the way, where is Tara?"

"She stayed quite late yesterday at the shelter, helping Vanessa with the animals, but I heard her stirring about earlier." Annie glanced through the kitchen screen, recalling how unusually quiet Tara had been since Carla's illness. If she hadn't acted quickly to get help for Carla, things could have turned out quite differently. But finding her had obviously been a shock for Tara.

As though she'd been summoned, Tara appeared at the screen door in her signature jeans and the same top she'd worn at her first Hook and Needle Club meeting. She traveled light, Annie realized, and made a mental note to offer some additions to her wardrobe.

"Good morning! Bring your coffee and come on out. Alice is here." Some of yesterday's tension had faded from Tara's thin face, but a haunted expression lingered in her eyes.

"Hi, Tara," Alice called, making room at the table.

Tara settled in a chair across from Annie and greeted them rather soberly, the shadows beneath her eyes pronounced in the sunlight.

"I called the hospital this morning," Annie said, reassuringly. "Carla's better. She's responding to the treatment, but the hospital will probably keep her another day or so." She paused, studying the face across the table. "Now, what about you? You look a little peaked today."

"I'm fine," Tara said, bringing the cup to her lips. "I didn't mean to sleep so long." An apologetic smile touched her lips, but it only heightened the melancholy that lingered there. Vanessa had been staying with her father for a few days and was unable to help, leaving the brunt of the work for Tara. She wasn't strong and likely had overworked.

"I should go out to the shelter this morning," Tara said, addressing no one in particular.

"I know the animals need to be fed," Annie said. "I'll go and give you a hand. That way you can be done in time for the meeting. You're making such progress. Before you know it, you'll be a champion knitter."

Tara nodded, but she looked distracted. Perhaps she was simply tired. She had kept busy designing flyers for the benefit and helping Annie with the cross-stitch canvases. In the evenings she would disappear into her room; Annie had missed their conversations over tea.

*   *   *   *

Annie and Tara arrived only minutes before Mary Beth called the Hook and Needle Club meeting to order. Mary Beth came in from the back of the shop carrying a large, high-sided box. Apparently, the first order of business would have something to do with the mewling, wiggling contents of the box. The kittens had outgrown the basket, from which they might easily have escaped.

Mary Beth drew the kittens out one by one as Kate quickly recoiled. "We'll get them out of here soon, Kate. I promise! Now, friends, it's time for each of these darlings to take up new residence. I hope some of you able-bodied ladies are willing to provide some of them a home, or help me find them one. You can pick up your kitten after the meeting." She cuddled each one and held it up for inspection before returning it to the box. The last kitten she brought out was the black runt of the litter.

Tara rushed over to Mary Beth, her eyes lighting up. "He's so sweet and so small!" she said softly.

Annie was glad that the kittens had taken center stage and deferred the inevitable questions about Carla that were sure to come. She watched Tara take the black kitten from Mary Beth's hands and hold it close to her cheek, stroking the soft fur.

"I'll take the little black runt," Annie said quickly, with a wink in Mary Beth's direction. What had she done? Boots could eat it for lunch! She'd have to keep a close watch until Tara left and took it with her.

Gwendolyn Palmer, who had once rescued two kittens and was a great supporter of animals, couldn't resist taking on another. Peggy chose a ragged black and gold female for Emily, whose birthday was only a couple of days away. Annie imagined the excitement on the little girl's face when she saw her present. She'd probably put a tutu on the poor thing and teach it to dance!

Only one kitten hadn't been claimed by the time the oohs and aahs were over, and the box containing the delightful little allergens had been removed to the back room. Everyone returned to their projects, buzzing with enthusiasm. Stella Brickson, who had barely paused in her knitting, viewed the proceedings over her rimless glasses. "Well, I guess that's one we'll have to consign to the dragon lady."

The others turned silent. Tara frowned and busied herself with the contents of her newly acquired tote bag. Annie realized that Stella had not heard the news about Carla's accident.

"Well, she's not breathing fire right now," Gwen said

with a knowing look and a slight toss of her elegant head. "She's in Stony Point Hospital. She picked up some disease from that owl she rescued."

Stella drew her lips together and clacked her needles with renewed vigor. The others began buzzing about Carla Calloway's mishap and how Tara had called 911.

"It must have been real scary for you," Peggy said, leaning over and touching Tara's hand lightly as she walked past.

Tara only nodded, frowning and drawing back from Peggy's spontaneous touch. Of all the members of the group, Peggy seemed most likely to elicit Tara's shyness. Odd, since the two of them were probably the closest in age. Annie watched Tara study the doggie blanket she was Mary Beth had been placed next to her, having been assigned to guide her progress. On the other side of Tara was Stella, who worked her own project with intensity.

Mary Beth leaned in to correct a stitch that had slipped off Tara's needle. "There, that should get you back on track," she said. Then, pausing, she added in a rush of curiosity, "What's she like? I mean, no one's gotten to know Carla or visited her house. I hear she lives in the back part of the old Bergner place and uses the rest for the shelter."

"Yes," Tara confirmed shyly. "She has a small sitting room and a kitchen and a bedroom in the back. I—I only saw it because ..." She broke off, her frown deepening. "I went to find her because I saw that the dogs hadn't been fed that morning. She was just lying there, moaning, and she looked awful. Her arm was all red and sore looking ..."

"Tara acted quickly," Annie put in, wanting to ease her tension. "She called for help, and then she and Vanessa took care of things at the shelter."

"I straightened up her room a bit, and put her sheets in the washing machine," Tara said, looking into the distance. She said no more but began stitching with studied intensity.

The others realized Tara didn't want to say any more and took up other subjects as they worked. Gwen and Peggy went to get coffee. That left just Alice and Annie at the table. Stella sat quietly to the side of Tara, perhaps feeling rebuffed for her comment about the hapless Carla Calloway.

"Don't mind them," Annie said gently when the others left the room. "They're naturally curious about the way other women live. We're each a bit of a busybody, you know." Looking down she saw that Tara's hands had stilled. She was chewing the inside of her lip thoughtfully. Two stitches dropped off her needle. "Are you all right?" Annie asked softly.

"Oh, it's just ..." She let the needles and the purple doggie blanket fall onto her lap. "I was just thinking ..." She stopped and began again. "When I was cleaning up, I found something Carla must have dropped. It was an old newspaper clipping, all yellow and crumbly. And a curl of hair dropped out of it. I know I shouldn't have, but I read it, and ... I just can't stop wondering about it."

"I heard Carla's not the neatest pin in the pack," Alice said lightly, shrugging to indicate that no malice was intended. "My mother used to save newspaper clippings too and put them in her scrapbook."

"What bothers you about it?" Annie asked, watching Tara closely.

"I don't know exactly." Tara's eyebrows drew together

in concentration. "It was from *The Point* here in town. Just a small notice about some teenager stealing a car and her mother coming to get her." She paused and added, "Her mother was killed on the way."

"How awful," Alice said softly.

"There was something inside the newspaper," Tara said, dark eyes widening. "It fell out. It was a curl of hair and a ring made out of beads—red, yellow, and blue."

"How curious," Alice murmured.

"Do you remember what the clipping said exactly?" Annie asked.

"I do remember," Tara said. "I've been thinking about it ever since …" She broke off, and then began reciting in a monotonous voice: "An unidentified teen was arrested earlier this week after stealing H.T. Simmons's car." She looked up at Annie. "It happened on Ocean Drive—near where you live. Do you know a Mr. H.T. Simmons?"

Annie searched her mind but nothing clicked. "No, I'm afraid I don't, but I haven't been here long, you know. But then, Carla is new to Stony Point too."

"Did you say Simmons?" It was Stella Brickson whose clacking needles had stilled. She peered over her narrow glasses in Tara's direction. "What were those initials again?"

"H.T.," Tara repeated. "That's all it said. H.T. Simmons."

Stella pursed her lips and was quiet for a moment. Her penetrating gaze went beyond the small circle of women, and then returned to focus on Tara. "My cousin on my father's side was named Simmons. Herbert Thorwald. He only lived here in Stony Point for a few years—had a passion for cars, the faster the better. I believe he headed for the Midwest—

Indianapolis to be specific. Why, I haven't thought of H.T. in years. We weren't close, you see, but ..." She broke off and cocked her head. "Why, imagine that woman saving a clipping about someone in my family."

The three other women stared at Stella, who'd returned to Stony Point late in life after many successful years showcasing artists in New York City. What could Carla Calloway have in common with Stella's cousin? Annie turned to Tara. "How old was the clipping, Tara?"

"I don't know. I looked for a date, but it wasn't there. It was just a circled paragraph, and around it was some stuff about the weather and upcoming events." She stared at Stella, still nibbling the inside of her cheek.

"Well, it has to be thirty or forty years ago," Stella said. "H.T., rest his soul, passed in 1990, but he was a young man when he left Stony Point. He took off for the Midwest well after I went to New York. I don't think he ever came back." She paused, searching the halls of her memory, and then returned to her knitting. But the frown etched in her forehead lingered.

"That's odd," Annie said. "Perhaps the two knew each other."

"Did your cousin have curly black hair?" Tara asked. "I mean ... really curly, like mine?"

"Certainly not," Stella said. "He was a towhead. His hair was so blond it was almost white, even as a teenager. Mind you, when he took off for the Speedway he'd lost most of it. The Simmons men were prone to early baldness."

"Well, then the hair couldn't be his, but maybe he gave her the ring. Maybe the two of them were ..."

When Stella glared over her glasses, and Tara didn't finish her sentence, Annie said, "You never know. History has an odd way of twisting and turning. Thirty or forty years is a long time. Stony Point must have all kinds of secrets." She gave Tara an apologetic glance. "Sadly, we haven't learned much about your mother yet."

"Well, I'm going to go through some of the Simmons archives," Stella said, pursing her lips once more and whacking away at her knitting. "I'm sorry that woman's ill, but I can't imagine what she has to do with my deceased cousin."

Annie rolled her eyes at Alice. Stella was a proud woman, as she supposed all New Englanders were, and it was no doubt natural that she wouldn't appreciate learning about her family from some outsider like the prickly Carla Calloway. But Annie knew Stella's straightlaced demeanor covered a heart as tender as rose petals. She'd throw in her share when they ordered flowers to be delivered to Carla's room.

"I—I shouldn't have said anything," Tara whispered to Annie when they gathered up their things and prepared to leave the shop. "Carla would probably fire me if she knew I'd told you all about the clipping. It's just that I feel sorry for her. She's so—I don't know—troubled. And she has been good to me."

And likely it takes one troubled soul to recognize another, Annie thought, regarding Tara's brooding eyes. Maybe Carla also recognized a fellow sufferer. Maybe that's why she was gentle with Tara when she was such a bear with everyone else.

"Don't worry," she said, "Stella's bark is much worse than her bite, and Alice and I won't say anything to hurt

Carla. We'd like to help her too. All of us would. That's why we're having the benefit for the animals. And speaking of animals, you'd better go collect little Blackie. Mary Beth won't let you out the door without your charge."

"You mean?" Tara started with a lift of her eyebrows.

"Yes, Blackie's for you. You can keep her in your room at Grey Gables, and when you leave you can take her along with you. Boots and I will have a little talk about this temporary arrangement. She'll behave herself. I won't let her swallow the poor thing."

"Oh!" Tara said, throwing her arms around Annie's neck. "I didn't know you were taking her for me." She drew back, her cheeks pink. She had not shown such affection before and seemed embarrassed now by her spontaneous reaction.

Annie linked an arm through Tara's. "The little runt needs a good home. I know you'll give it to her, Tara. Love and a bowl of milk now and then—that's all any of us really need. Come on. Mary Beth will be champing at the bit."

~ 16 ~

Tara walked along the beach and thought about all that had transpired since she'd come to Stony Point. Two days had passed since she brought Blackie home from A Stitch in Time. She was touched by the gift of the kitten and by the warmth of her new friends. It was generosity she could never have anticipated and trust she had no right to claim.

They all cared about her search for her mother's story, and they cared about Carla. How strange that the two were inextricably linked. Wonderingly, Tara played their conversation over in her mind.

"You found the clipping, didn't you?"

Carla Calloway had fixed her with wary eyes, favoring her bandaged arm as she sat behind her desk. Just released from the hospital, she probably should be in bed, but she had quickly resumed her duties.

"I—I didn't mean to pry," Tara stammered. "I was just cleaning up a little and …" She met her employer's gaze, trying to analyze the expression on her face.

Carla stood and walked to the window. She was silent for a long time, just looking through the glass. When she turned back, her eyes were misted with tears. "I thought it was just a coincidence—you looking so much like her. That day you came in, all the years melted away. *She* was here

again. We were both fifteen years old and walking along
Stony Point beach together, drinking lemonade with Mrs.
Holden, laughing and full of summer adventure ..." Her
voice caught, and Tara was frightened. She'd never seen the
feisty Carla Calloway cry.

What was she talking about? Had she left the hospital
too soon? Was she delirious again? Tara took a step forward
but faltered, wondering what she should do and what she
should say. But Carla shook her head slowly, moistening her
lips before she spoke again. "When Stella Brickson came to
the hospital to see me and showed me what she'd found, I
knew who you were."

Stella Brickson? Tara thought back to Tuesday's meeting of the Hook and Needle Club meeting. They had been
discussing the clipping. Everyone but Annie and Alice had
gone, but Stella had overheard, and she'd remembered H.T.
Simmons, the man whose car had been stolen and wrecked.
He was a distant cousin of Stella's. But what did that have
to do with Tara and her mother?

"She found the whole story in one of her old scrap-
books," Carla said, pausing and catching her lower lip
between her teeth.

Had Carla been arrested for stealing? Had her mother
perished in the crash when the police phoned with the
news? The terror of the experience would have marked
anyone who'd gone through it and made them sad and re-
sentful. No wonder Carla was so indrawn and suspicious.
But why was she telling her all this? "What story? I don't
understand," Tara stammered.

"She called herself Corky," Carla said in a near whisper.

"She had curly hair—dark and thick—and when it rained it coiled up like corkscrews all over her head. She called me Carlotta, and we were best friends." She drew her arms across her chest, cupping the injured one, and a sad smile trembled on her lips.

Tara shrank back, frightened—though of what she didn't know.

"She never told anyone," Carla continued in the same detached voice. "All those years, and she never told a soul." With her good arm Carla pulled something from the pocket of her jeans—an envelope. She opened it to show Tara the contents. It was the coil of hair and the small beaded ring that Tara had discovered in Carla's bedroom. She held them out to Tara with trembling fingers.

"I don't understand."

"She gave these to me; I've always treasured them. When you read the article, you probably thought I was the girl who was arrested. But it wasn't me." Carla's eyes widened, as though she saw something Tara could not see. "It was *your* mother—Claire ... my best friend, Corky. But *I* was the one driving the car. *I* crashed it into that tree. *I* ran away and just left her standing there to face the police alone. I didn't do the right thing because I was afraid."

Tara backed away, staring at the ring and the black coil of hair that was so like her own. So that was why she hadn't been able to put that clipping out of her mind—the sight of that hair. It had seemed alive, as though it could speak to her. She had been touching part of her mother's life, a part she had never known. A part that had marked her forever.

"It was your *grandmother* who died in the crash, Tara,"

Carla moaned. "All these years, I've been haunted by what happened. Your grandmother might be alive today if I had told the truth that day. Oh, Tara, I—I am so sorry. Please, don't ever let fear keep you from doing the right thing ... like I did."

The mother she'd neglected had come alive to her in those few moments. She imagined her as a teenager, lonely and afraid ... as she had been. Longing for love, as she had been, and looking in all the wrong places. Claire's mother had died because of a childish indiscretion on a summer day. But she had never revealed the truth about Carla. That had taken loyalty and love. If only Tara could tell her mother now how much she loved her—how she'd always loved her.

But it was all too late. Her mother was beyond her reach. She fought to understand her emotions. She didn't hate Carla. Carla and Claire had been young and adventurous; they had done something wrong, and their folly had resulted in unforeseen tragedy. Neither had told the truth. Perhaps if they had, their lives would have been very different. Each lived with their guilt, just as Tara was doing now.

"Don't let fear keep you from doing the right thing," Carla had said. But Tara was afraid. She hadn't told the truth from the minute she'd come to Stony Point. She should have admitted why she and Jem had come to Grey Gables. She should have asked for forgiveness—as Carla had. If only she could find the strength. ... She had run from Carla, fast and hard without stopping, leaving her alone at the window, supporting her injured arm.

Now as she walked with these revelations crowding her

mind, Tara saw Grey Gables just ahead, its facade tinted gold in the late afternoon light. How good its hostess had been to her. How trusting. Indeed, everyone in Stony Point had shown her kindness. They too must subscribe to Annie's creed: *A person can stay strong through trouble by doing what's right and by opening your heart to others.*

Tara paused on the same hill she had climbed that first night where she'd been given shelter in Annie's house. She hid behind a tree, the ache in her heart weighing her down. She was a fraud! What a mess she had made of things with all her lies.

She would speak to Annie now and tell her the whole truth. She was about to step away from her hiding place when Annie came out onto the porch, her blue dress twirling as she closed the screen door. The lowering sun turned her hair golden. She was beautiful—beautiful and good. Or was she beautiful because she was good?

Tara watched a car pull up the drive. It was Ian Butler, the handsome mayor she had met and liked immediately. But his piercing eyes had put her on guard, and she had been glad to stay in the kitchen while he and Annie talked on the porch. Now they were going somewhere together, perhaps to dinner. There would be no time to speak to Annie now. She would have to carry the burden of her deception a while longer.

When she saw them disappear into the distance, she stepped out from behind the tree and walked to the house— the lovely Victorian house that had been her brief but blessed refuge. Her eyes burned with tears when she saw the note on the kitchen table:

Missed you, Tara. Hope you enjoyed your day. I fed Blackie. Ham and potato salad are in the fridge for you. See you tonight.

She stared at the note a long time as Boots twined around her ankles. She could hear an insistent mewling coming from above. Blackie was waiting for her. She started up the stairs to her room, but heard something at the back door, a scraping or stamping of feet. Had Annie forgotten something? Tara retraced her steps to the kitchen. She opened the back door, weary from the day's climb and the heaviness of her thoughts.

Her heart leapt to her throat as Jem pushed his way into the kitchen. She hadn't seen him since that day in the woods, the same day she'd found Carla sick and disoriented. She thought he had left her for good this time. And she'd begun to be glad.

He closed the door behind him and leaned against it. He looked worn and disheveled, as though he'd been up a long time; dark circles ringed his eyes and stubble shadowed his jaw. Her heart melted; she wanted to throw her arms around him. Instead she sprang away. "You've got to go! Annie will be back any minute."

"No she won't. She just left." He stared at her with an expression she couldn't read. "She probably won't be back for hours." A smile played briefly over his lips and disappeared. "It's just you and me." He took a step toward her. "Didn't you miss me, honey?"

"What are you doing here?" she demanded.

"I came back for you," he said in that same urgent way. "I could never leave you. You know that." His eyes strayed from her face, roaming around the kitchen. "Nice place," he said dreamily, "but it's time to go. It shouldn't take you long to pack your stuff—" He broke off, and then moved past her into the kitchen.

She stared at him as he walked toward the stairs. His shirt had pulled away from his belt, and his shoulders drooped. His too-long hair straggled against his collar. *He has come back for me!* She thought he had gone for good, but he loved her. He must love her!

But something inside her knew; she recognized yet another lie she was telling herself.

He wanted her to pack her bag and take off. Just like that, with no goodbyes and no explanations. How could she do that to Annie, and to everyone who had befriended her?

"No, Jem," she said, stepping ahead of him. "I'm not ready to go yet. There are things I have to ..." The hard glitter in his eyes stopped her.

"I told you to call me J.C.!" he screamed angrily. "We're going, but first you're going to show me where those pretty pictures are. You didn't think I'd forget our plan, did you?"

She shook her head, suddenly aware of what she should have known all along. He didn't love her, but only wanted what he could take from her. "No!" she said, blocking his way. "I'm not going to do this. It's wrong. It would hurt Annie. It would hurt everyone who has been so kind to me. I couldn't ..."

He pushed past her and headed up the stairs. She scrambled after him, grabbing the tail of his shirt. "Please, Jem! I have some money ... you can have it ..."

He continued up the steps, stumbling a little, and pushed open the door to the attic. He turned around to face her, his face an angry mask. "Now get it!" He paused, stroking his jaw with grubby fingers. Tara saw that he'd bitten his nails to the quick. "No, I'll need more than just one. Get two. Get three."

"I don't know where they are," she lied. She'd helped Annie get the one named *Country Meadow Fantasy* ready for Ian. It was to be sold at a New York auction, and the proceeds given to the animal shelter.

Jem climbed the stairs to the attic, dragging Tara with him. He began pushing trunks and crates around, tearing at boxes and knocking them off shelves. "Either you show me, or I'll find them myself. I'll tear this place apart!"

The sound of crashing and tinkling shattered the air. Boots howled, and the kitten in her bedroom cried like a lost thing. "Stop!" Tara pleaded. "Please don't do this!" More boxes thudded to the floor. A doll with a china head clattered against a trunk, its head breaking in two.

"All right! All right!" Tara screamed. "I'll get it." She leaned back against a tall bureau and dropped her arms to her sides in defeat.

Triumph glittered in his eyes. "That's better! Now make it fast."

"I'm not sure where ..." she stammered. If she could just buy some time, someone might come. Maybe Annie would return. But what would happen then? Would Jem stop? Or would he ... ? She dared not finish that thought. If Jem were desperate enough, and drunk enough, he might hurt Annie. Was he drunk? He was mean enough to be.

She forced herself not to look where the framed canvases rested flat, carefully wrapped in brown paper and tied with twine. She played at opening drawers; she looked behind dusty furniture.

"Come on! Big pictures like the one in the Brown Library wouldn't be there!" Jem whined. His foot caught the rung of the ladder propped up against the wall. "Get up there and look!" he commanded, nudging her roughly toward the ladder.

She climbed slowly, reaching the shelf where the large needlework pieces were stored. "I don't see them," she said and started to back down the ladder.

"What's in the brown paper?" he asked, narrowing his eyes and peering up.

She stood stock-still on the ladder, her heart pounding, but she knew he'd guessed.

"Hand it down," he said, stretching his arms up. "And be careful."

Be careful. He had just torn through precious treasures that Annie's grandmother had preserved over a lifetime, and he was telling her to be careful! She was trembling with anger and fear as she grasped the edges of the large canvas.

"No, don't come down them steps yet. There's more up there. I seen 'em," he said, his innate poor grammar resurfacing. Jem balanced the first package against the adjacent wall and turned back to her. "Give me that one too." Even in the dark attic she could see his eyes shining with greed. "And that one!"

The shelf was stripped of its treasures, and her heart was stripped of the love she once had had for him.

Tara descended the ladder and began mechanically to clean up the mess Jem had made. Elizabeth Holden's beautiful handwork—hours of love and patience and skill—lost. Annie's inheritance stolen. It was all her fault. If only she'd never come. If only she had told the truth from the beginning.

"That's good, that's good," Jem muttered as she replaced fallen items tenderly. "We don't want the lady of the house suspecting anything until we're long gone. He began helping her, hastily returning boxes to their former positions. "OK, that's good enough. Now get your things. We're getting out of here."

Obediently, she left the attic and crossed to her room. She could see Blackie crouched beneath the bed, eyes wide in the tiny face. Jem followed her; he wasn't going to let her out of his sight. There was no chance to run or to use the phone. Sadness, anger, and regret scoured her heart. She was a wave-battered landscape after a storm.

She turned to look at him. "Jem, what would Wally think of you now?" she asked wearily.

He appeared stunned and grew silent. Several seconds passed. Then he gripped the door frame, his knuckles turning white. "He's a choir boy!" he said derisively.

"He's your brother. He cares about you," she said, placing her things in her yellow duffle bag and watching him. His lips trembled. She knew she'd struck a nerve. She had seen the look of admiration mixed with regret whenever Wally looked at Jem. She'd heard the childhood stories. Wally was respected in Stony Point, a hardworking part of the community. Now his brother was doing something that would hurt Wally and his friends deeply.

"Never mind the soft soap. Hurry up. We've got to make

tracks. The camper's out back in the woods behind this place. We have a little trekking to do."

She heard Blackie's frightened meow beneath the bed. It broke her heart, but she'd have to leave him here where it was safe. Annie would see that he was taken care of. "I want to leave a note. It'll just take a minute." She reached into the middle desk drawer for paper and a pen.

"Sure," he said sarcastically. "And tell her all about me? What do you take me for?" He reached to grab the pen from her grasp.

"I won't say anything about you; I just want to say good-bye." She bent over the desk, scribbled onto the blue paper: *I'm sorry. Thank you for everything. I'm so sorry. Tara*

"Sweet," he said mockingly. "Now, let's go." He picked up her heavy duffle bag, his face close to hers. He paused, stroking her cheek with his free hand. "It's just like we planned, baby," he said softly. "It's just you and me." Then he stepped across the hall and hefted the three wrapped canvases.

He didn't see her draw two small items from her pocket and place them on the dresser—a coil of dark hair and a small beaded ring.

~ 17 ~

The sun was sinking low on the horizon, softening the edges of everything when Ian drove away from Grey Gables with Annie. When he'd called her earlier that afternoon and proposed a visit to Carla's animal shelter, he hadn't been sure she would come.

It had been less than a week since he'd been out to Grey Gables. She'd served him lemonade and oatmeal cookies on the porch while Wally worked on the pantry shelves. It seemed like a month of Sundays had elapsed. *Ah, you're losing it, old boy.* But the truth was he looked forward to Annie Dawson's company with ever-growing anticipation.

She had answered with laughter in her voice. "Good afternoon, Mr. Mayor, sir!"

Drat those caller-identification monitors that allowed for no secrets. "That's what Peggy calls me, but I prefer Ian, especially when I'm not acting in my official capacity. How are you, Annie?"

"Right as rain, as Gram would say. Thankfully, the sun's shining on Grey Gables—at least for another few hours today."

"Speaking of Peggy," Ian began slowly, "I understand something happened out at the shelter. She said something about an owl, and Tara finding Carla unconscious."

"That's true, Ian. Carla was barely conscious and running

a high fever when she was found. She picked up some disease from that wild owl she's been tending, but she's much better … thanks to Tara's quick action."

He heard a note of pride in her voice; she'd become fond of the girl who'd appeared on her doorstep. Tending the wild and sick, it seemed, was something Annie and Carla had in common.

"I'd like to pay Carla a visit—to let her know that the town's supporting her," he said. "Any chance I could talk you into accompanying your mayor on a compassionate visit? Could I pick you up in an hour? I'll buy you supper afterward."

"Well …" She had hesitated, long enough to send his hopes plummeting. Then she said, "I haven't seen her since she got home from the hospital. Do you know she arranged for a taxi to take her home, rather than ask anyone to drive her?"

"That sounds like Carla. I have something to tell her that might perk her up, though. It's about licensing for the shelter. She might be ready for some good news." He paused, waiting for Annie to say something, but she remained quiet. Did she think it presumptuous of him to ask her to go with him at the last minute? She probably had plans for the evening—maybe even a date. Ian realized he was holding his breath.

"I did plan to get out there now that she's home." Annie had hesitated, and then added, "Having someone with me wouldn't hurt. Carla's not too talkative—at least not around me. But maybe we've softened her up a bit with the flowers the Hook and Needle Club sent."

He waited for her to make some excuse to turn him

down, but maybe he qualified at least as "someone."

"See you in an hour," she had said decisively.

When he pulled into her driveway, she was waiting on the porch, a blue vision against the white wicker chair. It was the color he liked best on her. It brought out the green in her eyes and heightened the color of her sunny hair. As she shouldered her purse and walked out to meet him, he wondered if she had any idea how beautiful she was.

"You look especially radiant this evening, Annie," Ian said. "I assume you still have a houseguest. Is she down at the shelter with Carla?"

"I don't know," Annie said. A shadow of worry lingered in her eyes as they drove toward the shelter. "She was gone when I got up, I haven't seen her all day."

When Annie and Ian arrived at the shelter a few minutes later, Carla was at her desk, a stack of papers spread out in front of her. A huge bouquet of purple and pink blooms nearly obscured her face. No doubt these were the flowers from the Hook and Needle Club; she'd thought enough of them to bring them back with her. She hadn't wasted any time resuming her duties. It was nearing seven o'clock in the evening, and she was still working. "Ms. Calloway," Ian addressed her, standing aside for Annie to enter.

"It's *Miss* Calloway," Carla said, looking up. She glanced from Ian to Annie. "I'm still what's known as an unclaimed treasure!" Humor or surprise edged out the caustic tone he'd come to expect from Carla.

"Hello," Annie said, taking the initiative, to his great relief. "Mayor Butler and I wanted to tell you how glad we are that you're better and to see if you need anything."

She peered at them curiously. Her gray hair had been pulled back from her roundish face; stray strands softened the severity of the style. She wore a button-down smock of lavender that made her look feminine, and almost vulnerable. Annie had never seen her stocky frame in anything but dark jeans and a flannel shirt.

Annie nodded toward the great bouquet a few inches to the side of the large desk. "It is a bit overwhelming, isn't it? But I hope you like it."

Carla's red-rimmed eyes, more gray than blue, moved to the flowers, and she studied them. She gave a little nod that might pass for appreciation, and then she looked down at her hands without speaking. She ran her tongue over her lower lip and looked up. "How is Tara?" Quickly she put her head down again, as though regretting an impulsive question.

"Tara's fine," Annie answered. "She was very concerned about you, though. Luckily, she found you and called for help. You were pretty sick."

"Blasted bird!" Carla said. Then her expression softened. "Gomer was just doing what wild birds do, I suppose." She paused for maybe a full thirty seconds, furrowing her brow. "The girl did all right on the website. She's smart." Her statements were stilted, as though she were unused to speech. "Didn't think she'd be worth her salt at first."

"Well, now you know better," Annie said. "Tara's relieved to know you're all right. And we all have been praying for you too."

At this Carla looked up sharply and narrowed her eyes as though trying to decipher a puzzle. Then she reached for a bottle of water that was making a wet ring on the stack of papers. "Mouth is dry as dust. Must be the medicine or something." When she put the bottle down again, she looked at Annie and asked in a subdued voice, "Did ... did she ... that is, did she say anything?"

Annie seemed at a loss to understand the question and left it dangling between them for an uncomfortable length of time. Ian took this moment to add his wishes for Carla's full recovery. "You're doing a good job for our community," he said. "I brought you some information from the state licensing board and the questionnaire you needed," he said, handing her a manila folder.

She took it and set it down slowly. She stared at it as though its contents could be revealed without opening it. Maybe she was just tired, Ian thought. Most likely she had to continue at home the treatments begun in the hospital.

"We're all glad to have you back on the job, but shouldn't you be resting?" Ian asked.

"Got some more strays to foist on me, aye?" she quipped in true Carla Callous fashion. But the sting wasn't in it, and Ian saw in those almost blue eyes a glimmer of humor or resignation or ... what? Something was different.

He gave Annie a look to indicate that they should go to allow Carla to rest. "Let me know if you need help with any of the details," he told Carla.

Ian watched Annie place her hands gently over Carla's folded ones and thought how comforting her touch would be.

When they reached the door, Carla's raspy voice came hesitantly. "Thank her for me—will you? Tell her I'm sorry."

Her? Did she mean Tara? And what was Carla apologizing for?

Annie turned with an apologetic smile. "I think you'll be able to do that for yourself, but she doesn't blame you. It was an accident, and she didn't mind looking after things while you were away."

Ian said goodbye to a pensive Carla and took Annie's arm. He drove slowly toward Maplehurst Inn, grateful to have her next to him, and the promise of the evening ahead of them. She seemed quieter than usual—preoccupied perhaps with all that had transpired—but Ian didn't press her to talk. Being with her was always easy—and special— whether they talked or not. Still, he hoped she knew he was there for her. He remembered the karaoke night at Sweet Nell's and singing *You've Got a Friend*. He'd sung it especially for her, and he'd meant it with all his heart.

"They have great pasta here," Ian said when they arrived at Maplehurst Inn. Inside the restaurant, he held her chair for her, aware of the subtle freshness of her perfume that put him in mind of beach roses and soft summer winds.

"Great for a girl's figure, especially at nearly eight o'clock in the evening," Annie said with a mock groan.

"Hardly a problem for you," he said, meaning it, and liking the slight blush that crept into her cheeks. He decided to relieve her embarrassment and changed the subject. "Carla seems rather impressed with your houseguest. The venerable guardian of animals hardly talked about anything else. She chases away most of the volunteers who come to the shelter. What do you think it is about Tara that's different?"

"I don't know," she said reflectively. "They seem to have some kind of bond. It's very odd. Tara says it's been like that from the start. Carla has always been gentle with her. She'd be giving someone all sorts of grief on the phone, but to Tara she'd be all sweetness and light. Sometimes she'd stare at her like she was trying to read her mind."

"Or maybe she was watching her like a hawk to make sure she wasn't sleeping on the job," Ian suggested.

"Imagine Carla thinking Tara would be upset with her for getting sick and having to leave everything in her hands. Wanting me to tell her she was sorry. I just can't figure out our Miss Calloway at all."

"Nor can I," Ian agreed. "I've never known her to apologize for anything."

"You know," Annie said, twirling her water glass in her hand, "Tara told me that while she was cleaning up Carla's room after the EMTs left, she found an old newspaper clipping by the bed. It was about a young girl visiting Stony Point who stole some guy's car. She took it for a joy ride and wrapped it around a tree. She wasn't hurt, but when her mother was coming to get her after the police phoned her, she was killed in an automobile accident."

"Tragic," Ian said. "Did it say who the girl was?"

"No, but the newspaper reported the name of the guy whose car was stolen—H.T. Simmons."

Simmons. The name was familiar, but to his knowledge there were no Simmonses around Stony Point any more. "I think there used to be a Simmons connected with Stella's family."

"Yes, so we discovered. Stella wasn't delighted at the prospect of being connected though."

"I can imagine," he said. "Well, it's a mystery." He wiped his lips with his napkin. "And speaking of mystery, has anything turned up about Tara's mother? That's why she's hanging around, isn't it?" He hadn't meant it to sound derogatory, but he caught Annie's quick frown. She was touchy on the subject of Tara.

They steered clear of Annie's houseguest for the remainder of their supper and drove to Grey Gables after dessert, which for him was chocolate cake. Annie ordered a more sensible raspberry sorbet. Her plan was for him to pick up a canvas for the auction in New York, which Stella had arranged. Stella's cousin, who ran the auction, had showcased other Betsy Originals with good success, and this one would benefit the animal shelter.

"It's a quick business trip," he said after parking the car. It was dark as they walked toward Grey Gables; only a handful of stars winked over the house. "I'll take the red-eye tonight and be back late tomorrow. I'll drop the canvas off at the gallery for you."

"Thanks, Ian. The last one netted almost $3,000. I can hardly believe it! Gram wouldn't believe it either. But I think she'd be pleased to know her work is benefitting the community." Annie turned the key in the lock. "Miss Boots has deserted me. She's usually here with the welcome mat out," she said. "She doesn't like prowling around after dark like a common Tom. But she's been acting a little weird since the advent of Blackie."

Ian followed Annie inside and shut the door. "Blackie?"

"One of the abandoned kittens Mary Beth found. It's Tara's kitten actually. She treats it like a princess and keeps it in her room when we're away."

Her room. Was Annie carrying hospitality a bit too far?

Was she setting herself up for disappointment? She had no good reason for mistrusting Tara, but something about her just didn't ring true.

Grey Gables lay in silence. Apparently Tara Frasier, who'd been gone all day, had still not returned. At the worried look on Annie's face, Ian felt quick vexation. The girl hardly expressed appropriate behavior toward a generous hostess.

"Come on up," Annie said. "The 24 x 36s are on the shelf in the attic. I wrote 'Country Meadow Fantasy' on top so it would be easy to identify for you. It'll just take a minute."

Ian switched on the light and guided Annie gently by the elbow as they climbed the stairs. The skirt of her blue dress swished softly as she moved, and Ian felt breathlessness not related to stair climbing.

"There you are!" Annie called as she opened the attic door. Boots leaped out, preened around Annie's legs, and stood looking at her with a disdainful expression.

"How'd you get in there?" She scooped Boots up in her arms and handed her over to Ian. "Talk to her while I get the picture." Ian sat down in the small settee in the hallway and stroked the cat's fur.

Suddenly he saw a tiny black shadow dart out of the bedroom adjacent to the settee—the girl's room. The door had been left partially open and the kitten had escaped. Boots hopped off his lap and gave chase. "Blackie's broken out and the National Guard's going after him!" he called to Annie, amused and hoping Boots's intentions were benign.

When Annie didn't respond, he returned to the attic doorway and saw her scrambling among boxes, pushing crates aside. She paused, her hand on the rungs of the ladder from which she'd just descended. She stared up at the shelves.

"Problem?" he asked, stepping inside. One look at her stricken face, and he was no longer amused by animal antics. "What is it?" he rasped.

"They're gone—the four pictures I put on the top shelf!" She'd turned as white as his Sunday shirt, and her eyes were filled with shock and hurt. She stared at him, her lower lip quivering. "Gram's beautiful needlework. It's gone!"

He took her in his arms, felt her trembling against him, and his heart seemed to crack. "Are—are you sure?" he whispered. And he felt her nodding her head against his chest.

In a few seconds she stepped back and drew her breath in sharply. She crossed her arms in front of her. "I'm—I'm sorry. It's just that I feel so—"

She didn't finish the sentence, but Ian knew precisely what she meant. She had been violated. Someone had taken something precious to her.

"They were here yesterday morning. I know it," she wailed. "And now they're simply gone." She dropped down on a large trunk. Ian stood above her, placing his hands on her shaking shoulders.

The attic was tidy—for an attic. He knew Annie had put in a lot of hours going through Elizabeth Holden's treasures. Had someone unknown broken in and stolen the canvases? The attic's windows were shut tight as a drum with no sign of entry. In his heart he knew the thief had to be someone who came and went at Grey Gables—someone who knew the canvases were there and knew of their value. Someone like Tara Frasier.

As though he'd voiced his suspicions aloud, she whispered, "She wouldn't! She wouldn't do this." Her imploring green eyes searched his. "Someone else must have …" She didn't complete her sentence but leaped up and ran down the stairs.

Ian followed her to the front door where they examined the lock and casing. No sign of jimmying, and the wood was unmarked. Together they hurried to the back door. It too was closed, though not locked. Obviously, the thief— and Ian had a pretty good idea who the thief was—had fled through the back of the house, taking the Betsy Originals with her.

"Who else comes and goes from Grey Gables beside Tara?" Ian said, the question more of a statement. "There's Wally, of course." He was sometimes short of money and had access to the house, but he was a trusted friend. Annie's friend.

"No," she said, "Wally wouldn't." She shook her head from side to side and sank down on a kitchen chair.

Ian wanted to shout or hit something. He'd find Tara Frasier and shake the truth out of her. He'd make her confess and return Annie's property. He pulled her toward him, held her, and felt her whole body go limp.

"Where is she? Where is Tara?" he demanded. Annie had taken the little fraud into her home, fed her, befriended her, and all the while she was snooping around, waiting for the right moment to steal from her!

"I don't know," Annie said barely above a whisper. "I didn't see her this morning. She was still in bed when I left. She's been so tired working extra hours while Carla was in the hospital. Last night she didn't even want supper when she came home."

As though on telepathic cue, they both headed for the guest room—Tara's room. Ian pushed the door all the way open, and they stepped inside. The bed was made, the room neat and orderly, as though freshly prepared for a new guest's arrival.

Annie rushed to the closet, staring in with that same shocked, sorrowful look that tore at Ian's heart. "Her things are gone," she said in a small voice. "She didn't have much, but it's all gone—her yellow duffle bag—everything." She paused as the little black kitten scampered into the room and leaped onto the white bedspread. "Everything," she repeated, "except Blackie."

"Annie," he said, wishing he could comfort her but finding no words.

"She loved that kitten. Why would she leave it behind?"

Ian gritted his teeth. The girl had pretended to care about Annie too, but it had all been an act—an awful joke. "We have to call the police," he said, pulling out his cellphone.

"No. Wait. Not yet," Annie said, turning toward him. Then rushing past him she picked up something from the pine dresser. A small square of white paper. She read it out loud, her lips pale and trembling.

"I'm sorry. Thank you for everything. I'm so sorry."

"That's it?" he heard himself say incredulously. "She steals art worth twelve to fifteen thousand dollars, and she's *sorry*?"

Annie shook her head. "I just don't understand it. How can she hope to sell them? Any gallery would check the provenance of the artwork. Tara's too smart to think she could get away with this. Besides, how could she do it? She doesn't have a car. She either walks or takes my bicycle to the shelter. And I saw the bike when we came home tonight."

Ian drew in his breath and ran a hand through his hair. Of course, she couldn't hop on a bike with four huge needlework pieces in heavy frames. She had to have access to a car, or to someone with a car. She had to have an accomplice. "Has she made any friends here yet?" he asked, trying to keep the anger out of his voice.

"Only the girls at the Hook and Needle Club." She crossed her arms over her chest as though the summer night was cold. A tear rolled down her cheek. "She was learning how to knit."

"Come on," he said, pulling her gently by the arm. "We'll go talk to Reed." Reed Edwards, the chief of Stony Point's small police department, had an office just down the hall from Ian's. Annie trusted him; maybe she'd feel better talking to him in person. But regardless of what happened, Ian wasn't about to leave her alone at Grey Gables tonight. He'd call Alice and arrange for Annie to stay with her.

"Wait. Look. She left something." Annie picked up a small bead ring from the dresser where she'd found the note. Next to it lay what looked like a coil of hair.

Ian stared at them in confusion. They were the items Annie had spoken of—things she said Tara had found in Carla's bedroom.

"I want to stop by the shelter first, Ian," Annie said with sudden force. "Maybe she's there. Maybe she's trying to tell me something by leaving those things behind ..." But the sentence trailed off.

Ian wanted to fix this—and fix it right now. He wanted to go after Tara Frasier before she got away. They'd likely lost valuable time already. "What good would it do to go to the shelter?"

"Please, Ian," she said, her heart in her eyes.

There was no way he could deny her. They closed the bedroom door and went downstairs together.

— 18 —

Jem prodded Tara out into the gathering night, pressing the framed canvases against her back. "Move! Head for the woods and don't stop." His voice was high with excitement, and he panted with exertion.

Tara struggled with her duffle bag, her feet slipping on the cobbled walk. The moon paled in the not-yet-black sky, and crickets had begun to mourn the dying day. She shivered in her light blouse and the shorts she'd worn that long day as she roamed the beach and rocky coast of Stony Point. There'd been no time to change and no time for a last look at the lovely old house. She'd had no chance to give Blackie one last cuddle.

She would have to go with Jem and carry out his plan. He expected her to do just what he said ... as she always had. He snapped his fingers and little Tara would come running. She'd stumble after him and go where he wanted her to go. And she would leave another piece of herself behind that could never be recovered. She was so tired.

As she pushed forward through the lengthening grass with Jem close on her heels, the faces of her Hook and Needle Club friends flashed before her: Mary Beth, patiently guiding her fingers on the oversized knitting needles, and Alice, with gentle eyes and jingling bracelets, praising her designs and urging the adoption of her little feral kittens. Tara thought of Peggy—all innocent eyes and sweet smiles pledging a friendship that she, Tara, had refused. And there was Gwen and Vanessa and Kate ... how kind each of them had been. Even Stella Brickson, who had seemed so severe and so uncompromising, had welcomed Tara in her own way; she too had tried to help.

"Not much farther now!" Jem panted.

They plunged into the dark trees. Thick shrubs scraped her face and thorny twigs clawed at her bare legs. Startled birds flapped and squawked as their woodland sanctuary was invaded. The county road on the other side of the forested strip had to be where he'd hidden the old conversion van with its fading paint and dented sides. She knew he was ashamed of it; that's why he showed up in Stony Point with a fancy rental car. J.C., the successful businessman, couldn't be caught dead in a wreck like that.

They'd believed him and had accepted that well-groomed, well-spoken facade. He'd fooled them—even Wally who looked at his brother with such sad affection. One could live on lies carefully chosen, carefully maintained—for a while. Then it would all come tumbling down, and the bricks would fall on the innocent. Tara thought of Annie—dear Annie. Tara could barely swallow for the rising flood of tears.

Suddenly she saw the decrepit old van that had been turned into a camper. It leaned oddly to one side where the ground was uneven. She slowed her steps, not only because she was exhausted, but because the thought of getting in it with Jem filled her with revulsion ... and fear.

"Come on!" he rasped, pressing the hard frames into her back once more.

Jem was such a fool at times, so blind. How could he hope to sell original art pieces without someone checking their origin? "This is crazy! We'll never get away with this, Jem ..."

He misunderstood. "Nobody knows about this old rig. I've kept her hidden in a beat-up old trailer park in Petersgrove until now. They'll never look for us in it!" He pressed up close to her. "Here, grab the keys. Open the back."

She fumbled in his pocket. It was damp and hot, and she felt his sweating thighs through the thin material. Shaking, she pulled out a lone key with a rabbit's foot attached to the chain. Insane laughter bubbled inside her. No one carried such a talisman anymore; but Jem swore by it. Poor, unlucky Jem!

"Quick. Back there!" He gestured for her to open the double doors at the back end of the vehicle. "That's it." He flung his cargo inside and jerked his head toward the driver's door. "Now, go start it up. And kill the lights!"

He wanted her to start the engine while he arranged the canvases; then he would climb in, and they would be off. He called the shots; little Tara would obey. She understood all this in seconds.

Something rose in her like a periscope out of the ocean. She scrambled behind the wheel and gunned the engine. It started immediately—a rare occurrence for the aging machine—just as Jem closed the double rear doors and started around to the passenger door.

Only Tara didn't wait.

Stamping hard on the gas, she roared up the ridge and onto the road, praying no car would slam into her. She could see Jem waving his arms behind her and heard his angry shouts, no longer muffled lest someone hear, but reckless and loud.

What was she doing? Where could she go? Her heart beat like a hundred jackhammers. It had been years since she'd driven a car. The thing lurched and growled so noisily that she was sure everyone in Stony Point could hear. They'd come after her. They'd find Annie's stolen canvases in her possession. For now, they were safe from Jem's grasping hands. But where could she take them? What should she do?

"Don't let fear keep you from doing the right thing."

Suddenly she thought of Carla's last advice to her. The shelter wasn't far; she knew the way, having walked or ridden Annie's bike to the animal shelter so many times. Two miles. She could get there and call someone. Annie? The police? They weren't likely to believe her. She could be arrested! Maybe Jem would even report that she'd stolen his vehicle and call the law in an ironic twist of madness!

Everything could come crashing down—all the false hopes, all the lies! But she was through pretending. She was going to do the right thing.

She drove on until the line of pens at the rear of Carla's property appeared. The van might be hidden from the road there! She cut the lights, which in spite of Jem's order she had turned on when lurching onto the road. The dogs began to bark. She scrambled out the driver's door and frantically called out to calm them. They knew her voice; perhaps they would stop before Jem got close enough to hear, if he guessed where she went.

Would he guess? Would he follow her here? If he ran

straight for the shelter it wouldn't take him long. Was she putting Carla in danger too? The seconds flew; the seconds dragged. Time was meaningless—only her fear and her determination were real. Annie must not be robbed of her treasures!

"Don't let fear keep you from doing the right thing!"

Carla's words, so fresh in her mind, rang in her ears as she banged her fists on the door. Carla might be sleeping, or she just wouldn't open the door. She would simply holler for whoever it was to go away. Tara gasped for breath and shivered beneath the pale moon. She'd be left on the sagging shelter porch that offered no shelter!

"Tara!"

She felt herself falling into the room. Then she was caught in a pair of strong arms.

"What is it, girl?" Carla's voice—sharp, yet kind.

"Lock the door! Turn out the lights!" she croaked, pressing further into the front room turned office where Carla stood, dressed in rumpled blue shirt and jeans.

"What is it?"

Tara raced to the hallway where she nearly collided with Boomer, the old dog who seldom barked. Recognizing her, he nudged his wet nose against her knee. Carla followed, and the two women and the dog huddled there.

Tara struggled to compose herself. "I—I didn't know where else to go." Haltingly, she explained how she'd been forced to steal needlework from Annie's attic, and how she'd left Jem and raced away in his camper. "Annie's things are in Jem's old van parked behind the pens. "I don't know what to do now, but I couldn't let him take them."

"Has he followed you?" Carla asked, pale brows furrowed over eyes that were amazingly sharp even in the darkness.

"I don't know!" Tara wailed, feeling the wave of panic roll over her once again. "It's all my fault." She blurted out the whole story of how she'd come to Stony Point with Jem for the purpose of stealing from Annie. How she'd tried to make Jem change his mind. How she hated herself for all the lies. "Annie's gone with Mr. Butler somewhere ... I don't know when she'll be back."

"We've got to find her—tell her what's happened." Carla brushed hair back from her face and chewed the inside of her cheek. "You're a brave girl, Tara." She said this with a kind of awe or pride or something Tara couldn't describe. Of course Carla would understand—she who had suffered so long over her own mistakes. "Now, listen to me. It's going to be all right." She looped her arm through Tara's. "My phone's in the office. Do you know the num—"

But Carla's words suddenly died when a raucous barking erupted from the dogs outside. Then came the banging of fists and rattling of the office door. Boomer gave a low, asthmatic growl but remained by Carla's side. Tara felt her heart leap to her throat. Jem had found her. He was here! They were trapped—an aging convalescent and a skinny, weak girl!

"Hush!" Carla said, directing her words to both dog and girl. She drew her arm around Tara's shoulder and held her still. "Does he have a gun?" she whispered as calmly as she could.

"I don't know! I don't think so, but he's mean—"

"Quick—into my bedroom! There's a lock on the door."

Carla herded her down the hallway, pushed her inside and drew the bolt across the door. She grabbed Boomer's collar, holding him against one hip while drawing Tara to the other.

There was more banging and then the shattering of glass. Tara cringed, wishing she knew how to pray. It would be only a matter of seconds before he would be inside. Everything was tumbling down, down.

~ 19 ~

Clutching the bead ring and the coil of hair, Annie's mind raced. Why had Tara done it ... if she had? And why was she ready to assign blame to the girl without proof? And yet, Ian was right. Who else knew where to look? The attic hadn't been torn apart. The thief had known exactly where the large originals were and had taken only them.

She reached for Ian's hand when they stepped out the front door. Darkness had fallen over Grey Gables, and the woods beyond were shrouded in a black cloak. She was glad he was with her, and that she had said yes to dinner and his company. At least she hadn't been alone to discover the theft of Gram's beautiful canvases.

"We'll take my car," Ian said.

Just as they were about to get inside it, they heard a motor. Someone was coming up the driveway. "Look, Ian." Annie stood frozen, watching as the truck approached and pulled to a stop. Wally hopped out.

"Evening, Annie," he called, walking around to the back of his truck, smiling. "I hope it's not too late, but I wanted to unload this lumber for the pantry. Got another load to bring in the morning ..." His voice trailed off as he looked from one to the other, dark eyes puzzled. "What's wrong?"

She stared into the familiar tanned face, the hair that

seldom stayed in place, the quick, dark hands on the back of his pickup. Frozen, she was unable to respond.

"Someone got into Annie's house," Ian said, eyeing the bed of Wally's truck. "Some of the Betsy Originals are gone."

Wally said nothing. He put his hands slowly into his pockets. A look of hurt crept into his eyes.

Annie shook her head. It was ridiculous to suspect Wally. He wouldn't steal a bottle cap. Besides, if he were guilty, he wouldn't nonchalantly drive up to her door. "Wally, do you know where Tara is?"

He stared at her, and then at Ian and back again. He ran a hand over his unruly hair. "Tara?" he repeated.

"We think Tara may have taken them," Ian said, "but someone had to—that is, she would have needed wheels, and ..." He let the sentence drop.

"Oh, Wally, we know you wouldn't do anything like this," Annie broke in. "It's just that ..." But she didn't know how to express the rush of disjointed thoughts leaping through her mind, and she hated the look that spread slowly over Wally's face. Hurt, fear ... what?

He seemed to be sorting out his thoughts, trying to comprehend what the two of them were thinking. He shifted his feet on the gravel and looked off toward the strip of forest behind them. He cleared his throat, swallowed. "I don't know where Tara is," he said slowly, "but there is something you should know—" Wally hung his head, shifted his feet once more. "I think she knows my brother Jem."

Of course she knew him. They'd met at her place, Annie thought. Tara hadn't liked him. She had seemed afraid of him. What could Wally be talking about?

"Jem is—he—uh ..." Wally sucked in air, let it out in a rush. "I think he might be the one who took the money from the Gas N Go. And then the other day I was watching for birds, and I saw him with her." His voice rose incrementally, and he brought his hand down hard on the pickup's fender. Anger or frustration or shame replaced the hurt on his face.

Jem? The charming man who'd regaled them with stories about Stony Point and fishing as a boy? The one who called himself J.C. and had a flourishing real estate business? Wally's brother, Jem? Annie was utterly perplexed.

Jem was with Tara. The accomplice Ian had suggested! Annie stared into Wally's stricken face. She heard Ian expel a long breath. He'd want to head for the police station right now, and that's probably what they should do. She felt the bead ring and the coil of hair still clutched in her left hand. What did it all mean? And what did Carla have to do with it?

She grasped Ian's hand more firmly. "Thank you for telling us, Wally," she said. "We'll find Tara. We're going to stop at the animal shelter. She's been working there, you know." And she walked away, leaving Wally standing there. She pulled a startled Ian toward his car.

They took the county road that wended along the woods, skirting the bluff. The bay nestled below, its deep waters brooding. In the light, it could be a pleasant drive with the sun shadowboxing through green leaves, but now its deep gloom matched Annie's dark thoughts. Ian drove in silence, his strong hands on the wheel giving her comfort as she focused on them.

They reached the sprawling property generously

furnished with pines and deciduous trees. The road forked sharply, and the old farmhouse appeared in the distance. They drove past the outbuildings and discarded farm implements, which Carla no doubt had inherited when she bought the place. There was even a motley-looking camper someone had abandoned behind a remote shed. They drove by the chain-link fences to the accompaniment of restless barking. One thing was for sure: No one was likely to sneak up on Carla unannounced.

The place lay in darkness—not even a porch light was in evidence.

"You suppose she goes to bed with the chickens?" Ian asked.

Ian pulled up alongside the dark farmhouse. Annie didn't wait for him to come around to her door but leapt out, shutting it noisily behind her. The dogs, having sounded their displeasure, quickly resumed their innocent pursuits. Stillness lay over the property like a pall.

"Eerie," Ian commented drily.

Her thoughts exactly, but she hurried up the dirt path and rapped on the door firmly and then more insistently, but no sound came from within. Had Carla gone out for the evening? Maybe she'd had a relapse and had to be hospitalized again. Random thoughts raced through Annie's mind. She welcomed them to cover the insistent sense that something was terribly wrong.

Ian moved off the porch and started around to the back. She raced after him, peering into dark windows that revealed nothing at all.

At the back of the house he stopped so abruptly that she

bumped into him. "See that window—that high one?" Ian whispered. "It's been broken!"

She followed his gaze and saw the jagged hole. But the window was a small one. Even fully broken out it wouldn't accommodate an adult, even a diminutive Tara. It could even have been an old break Carla hadn't gotten around to fixing.

Ian had moved ahead of her again. He spread his hands out signaling her to be quiet.

"What is it?" she whispered. But she saw what he was looking at. The screen door had been torn away, and the wood around the inside door shattered.

Ian pulled her away from the entrance and around to the side of the house. "Someone's broken in here!" His dark eyes grew bright, almost translucent and darted from her face to the door and back again.

"Oh, Ian!" she exclaimed. What could it mean? Why hadn't she let him call the police when he wanted to? He was digging in his pocket for his cellphone when they heard a loud crack like something falling or a door banging. Was Carla in trouble? Without a second's further thought Annie pushed through the door.

They entered a dark and damp mudroom, and then ventured into the kitchen. Neither spoke, their ears attuned for the slightest sound. But all was deathly still. Beyond the kitchen a narrow hallway loomed. When Annie stepped toward it, Ian pulled her back wordlessly and crept in front of her.

They moved stealthily. Suddenly there was a scuffle off to their left behind a closed door. Excited yips of a dog followed. Someone let out a cry, words she couldn't understand.

As one, she and Ian pushed against the door. Locked! Then suddenly it gave way and they nearly fell inside to find Tara on her knees, her hand on the knob. Carla was huddled against the bed, scrambling to get up. The chocolate Lab whimpered and wriggled his spastic hip in pitiful commiseration.

Annie looked from one to the other in astonishment and confusion. Tara's face was chalk white and streaked with dirt or tears or both. Her blouse was torn and angled over one pale shoulder.

"What's going on here?" Ian demanded, helping Tara to her feet.

"That wretched man is getting away! That's what's going on!" Carla sputtered. "He just took off through the front door when you came in the back!" Carla tested her balance, steadying herself on the dresser.

"Who? What man?" Ian thundered.

"Oh, Annie! It's my fault," Tara cried. "I tried to make him understand. Jem wouldn't listen."

Annie looked around for Ian, who had bolted out of the room. Where had he gone?

"It wasn't her fault!" Carla fumed. She smoothed her rumpled shirt with quick, angry strokes. "Now let's go to the office where we can talk!" Carla grabbed hold of the dog's collar. "Settle down, Boomer," she ordered. "Come on, Tara—Mrs. Dawson."

Annie and Tara followed meekly behind Carla who switched on the lights in the office, revealing the big round table with its clutter of papers and mugs. There was a computer and a file cabinet in one corner and an empty birdcage in another. Carla pulled out chairs, gesturing for them to sit.

"First thing you need to understand is that Tara tried to stop him. He forced his way into your house and made Tara get those canvases your grandmother made—those valuable ones we've all been hearing about." Carla stood near the computer, and with hands on her ample hips she matter-of-factly outlined all that had happened. She might have been a CEO explaining a business plan to company managers. "Tara got the key to his van and took off with the goods. She left Mr. Smarty Pants in the dust out in the woods and came to me for help."

Tara sat with her eyes on her lap, tears streaming down her cheeks. But Carla wasn't through.

"She thought that no-account had left town and had given up his greedy little plan, but as it turns out ..." Carla stopped for a breath. She sounded tough, but she looked shaken and pale. "She was afraid he'd follow her here, so she hid his vehicle behind the dog cages. She didn't want anything to happen to your things, Annie."

Annie listened with astonishment, especially when Carla revealed the reason why Tara had come to her—what the ring and the coil of hair were all about. It was an incredible story.

"Now, when our good mayor catches up with Mr. Jeremiah Carson, he'll show him a thing or two!" Carla finished with a flourish.

Annie clutched her hands in her lap. That's where Ian had gone! He'd gone after Jem; he was out there in the darkness. *Dear God*, she prayed silently. *Help him, please!*

～ 20 ～

Back at Grey Gables, Wally had watched Ian drive away with Annie beside him. He jammed his hands in his pockets, tearing the left one at the seam. He should have known! Jem hadn't changed. The way he had snooped around Grey Gables, asking about who visited, what went on there, and passing himself off as some kind of big tycoon. Peggy thought he was right up there next to Donald Trump!

The times he'd come into town on foot, the rundown shoes, hair too long … all these should have been clues. But Wally hadn't wanted to put it together. He wanted to believe Jem had made something of himself, but he was still looking for a quick buck, thinking only of himself. He hadn't denied taking the money from the Gas N Go either. He had just shaken it off as though it was nothing. But it was something.

And that load of garbage about just happening to run into Tara by accident along the coast road. It hadn't made sense to him then, but he'd let it go. He and Tara had probably planned the whole thing together. They'd both shown up around the same time. It was no coincidence.

Why had he not seen it? Did he need to be hit over the head with a two-by-four? Feeling sick, Wally climbed into his truck and put it in gear. Not sure what to do, he sped off in the direction Ian and Annie had gone. He had to tell them what he knew. He had to warn Annie about Jem and to help if he could.

It was darker than pitch along the road Ian had taken. Wally flipped on his high beams and headed in the same direction, hoping he wouldn't blind some poor driver coming the other way. But the world seemed to be sleeping. He slowed as he neared the property Carla had purchased to house all her strays. The trees grew thicker, arching over the road until their leafy tips joined. Why were Annie and Ian going to the animal shelter?

And suddenly something caught his eye. Just beyond an abandoned shed with a caved-in roof he saw a van or part of a bus. He let off the gas and peered into the trees that surrounded around the vehicle. It was old and dilapidated with dents that had been sanded and patch-painted with an amateurish hand.

Wally gaped. It wasn't a van or a bus, but some home-made rig. He'd seen it before—in Petersgrove!

He switched to low beams and pulled up behind it. The driver's door stood open. Suddenly someone jumped out and stood squinting in the glare of headlights. Wally knew who it was even before he saw the familiar muscular frame and the dark hair curling on the collar of his blue silk shirt. But what was Jem doing at the animal shelter?

"You lost, Jem?" he asked, drawing alongside and propping an arm on the camper door.

After a deer-in-the-headlights stare, relief flooded the dark features. "Hey, bro! You're a lifesaver." Jem grasped his brother's hand, sweat and fear palpable in his eyes. "Can't get her started." He glanced over his shoulder and then back again at Wally. "I need a lift." He darted furtively toward the rear of his camper. "Got an important delivery to make."

Wally blocked his brother's path, knowing exactly what "delivery" Jem had to make. "Nope." Jem stared through red-rimmed eyes. He opened his mouth, but no words came. "I'm not taking you anywhere," Wally said, staring Jem down. "I think you've got Annie's property in there. You're gonna give it back." Wally's pulse raced, shame and anger building inside him. "And where's Tara? What'd you do with her?"

Jem's low curse fell between them. "I don't have time to argue. We're leaving here." He grabbed Wally's arm in a fierce grip.

Wally shook it off. "I'm not some little kid following you around anymore!" Wally spat the words through gritted teeth. "You're a fraud. You came back here to lie and steal." Wally felt anguish rising, dreaded tears forming. He swallowed them, steeling himself. "I'd have done anything you asked, man. You're my family. I'd have given you anything—but not this way. No more, Jem. You gotta face up to what you've done and stop. Just stop!"

Seconds seemed like hours as he faced his brother. Maybe, just maybe he could get through to him.

Jem's grip on his arm loosened, but a crafty gleam replaced the fear in his eyes. "Now who's gonna believe you if they find the stuff in your truck? I'll say you and me were in it together. What do you think of that, bro?"

"I'll tell you what I think of that." Ian Butler appeared from behind a clump of bushes directly behind the spot where Jem stood. Moonlight glinted on his silver hair, and his eyes flashed like lasers in the night.

Jem leapt away, but Ian was on him in a second and took him to the ground.

Wally heard the wail of sirens and knew it was over for Jem. It was over, but he couldn't stem the rise of tears that stung his eyes.

— Epilogue —

"You don't have to leave," Annie said as she and Tara drank tea in Grey Gables's cozy kitchen.

"Thank you," Tara said with tears in her eyes. "Everyone's been so kind to me—especially you. You helped me find the strength to do the right thing. I'll never be able to thank you enough." She looked down at Blackie curled up in her lap. "But I have to go back; I need time to figure out my next step. I may go back to school. I want to make something of myself, prove I can do it."

"But you'll come back to see us," Annie said, swallowing the lump in her throat. "Everyone wants you to come to the benefit show this autumn. You've worked hard on it—all those cross-stitch canvases you framed, and the posters you designed."

Tara nodded, smiling. "Carla made me promise. I never would have learned so much about my mother without her." She lowered her head and stroked Blackie's fur. After a few minutes she looked up, eyes misty. "What do you think will happen to Jem? I'm not going back to him," she added hastily. "But still, I'm sorry for him—and for Wally."

"It will be up to the authorities," Annie said. "Jem will have to face up to what he's done. But my bet is that Wally won't stop trying to move his brother in the right direction."

She pushed the tea service aside. "But we can't be late for your last meeting of the Hook and Needle Club. Come on, get your tote, and let's go!"

* * * *

High excitement reigned at A Stitch in Time. Peggy, face glowing, had begged off work extra early and settled herself in the comfy circle of women. As always, she tossed off her shoes the minute she plopped down in a chair. When she opened her tote to pull out her quilt blocks, Annie saw the top of a pink-ribboned package. "Cover that up or take it to the back room. Alice will be bringing Tara back any minute."

Kate hadn't emerged yet from the kitchen where Annie knew she was bustling about getting things ready. Vanessa would bring in the cake at the last minute, excusing herself briefly to run next door to The Cup & Saucer where the chocolate confection would be waiting. Mary Beth, usually the voice of business, looked like she'd swallowed the proverbial canary. With wistful eyes, she murmured, "We'll all miss her."

Gwen had been charged with picking out a gift from all the Hook and Needle Club members, but Annie knew there would be the little extras. In spite of Tara's original intent, she had proved herself worthy. They had all seen the change in her, even before her flight from Jem with the stolen canvases. They had forgiven her. Now she was leaving Stony Point, going back to her apartment in Portland.

Annie smiled as she stitched with her crochet hook.

In a few minutes Alice, who'd invented an excuse to whisk Tara away for a few minutes, would return, and the party would begin. They'd gather around Tara and yell, "Surprise!" Annie looked around the circle, grateful for the warmth and understanding of these friends who meant so much to her.

She'd been asked to repeat the story several times. Peggy loved the part where Wally stopped his brother and refused to let him get away. "And Mr. Mayor actually flattened Jem?" she'd asked, wide-eyed.

Annie tried not to blush when they talked about how brave their mayor was. "Why, he was like a knight in shining armor," Vanessa said, "and you were the lady in distress he rescued." She beamed at Annie, as Annie's face reddened. "Well, three ladies, I guess … you and Tara and Miss Calloway."

Stella knitted away furiously on a beige wrapper. She wasn't saying much, but every once in a while she peered over her glasses toward the door. Annie was betting she couldn't wait to shout, "Surprise!" too.

"Isn't it amazing how Carla turned out to be Tara's mother's friend?" Gwen remarked. "All those years she never told anyone that she'd been driving that stolen car. Bet she won't be so callous now that she's relieved her conscience and told the truth. And she ended up helping Tara in the bargain. What a gift. It's amazing!"

Annie could hear Alice chattering to Tara just outside A Stitch in Time. Bracelets jingling, she'd open the door any second, giving Tara a little shove inside, and then they would descend on her with their gifts and their love. Annie couldn't keep from smiling as she watched with her dear friends around her.

Yes, she thought, *grace is always amazing ... the most amazing thing.*